The

WOLSENBURG
CLOCK

The

WOLSENBURG
CLOCK

[signature]

JAY RUZESKY

thistledown press

Thistledown Press Ltd.
633 Main Street
Saskatoon, Saskatchewan, S7H 0J8
www.thistledownpress.com

Library and Archives Canada Cataloguing in Publication

Ruzesky, Jay, 1965-
The Wolsenburg clock / Jay Ruzesky.
ISBN 978-1-897235-62-1

I. Title.
PS8585.U99W64 2009   C813'.54   C2009-904212-6

Cover and book design by Jackie Forrie
Printed and bound in Canada

Thistledown Press gratefully acknowledges the financial assistance of
the Canada Council for the Arts, the Saskatchewan Arts Board, and the
Government of Canada through the Book Publishing Industry Development
Program for its publishing program.

 Canada Council
for the Arts
Conseil des Arts
du Canada

 SASKATCHEWAN
ARTS BOARD

 Canadian
Heritage
Patrimoine
canadien

The

WOLSENBURG
CLOCK

For Tricia

Contents

11   Prologue

23   The Medieval Clock — 1378

57   Entr'acte

65   The Renaissance Clock — 1585

103   Second Intermission

113   The Enlightenment Clock — 1809

163   Epilogue

... by mediacioun of this litel tretys, I purpose to teche the a certein nombre of conclusions ...

— Geoffrey Chaucer, *A Treatise on the Astrolabe* (1391)

Whoever ... can no longer wonder, no longer marvel, is as good as dead ... A knowledge of the existence of something we cannot penetrate, our perceptions of the profoundest reason and the most radiant beauty, which only in their most primitive forms are accessible to our minds: it is this knowledge and this emotion that constitute true religiousness.

— Albert Einstein, *Ideas and Opinions* (1954)

Prologue

When I was offered the chance to look into the workings of the Wolsenburg astronomical clock, I accepted with the sense of delight a child has at a whirring, spinning thing. How could I have known the clock would take over my life, and that I was being offered the chance to look into the mind of God?

Wolsenburg is a small Austrian city near the Italian border and I happened to be there for what had been conceived as a brief retreat. I was staying at the modest home of an acquaintance I'd met at a conference at the Courtauld Institute in London. I had been there to give a paper on Mayan scribes and the patronage offered by the Howler Monkey Gods. I told him that I very much wanted to visit his city as it housed a document which had captured my attention and he immediately offered me his flat in his absence in return for the favour of feeding his cat, Schpatz, thereby relieving his disagreeable neighbour temporarily from the chore. I prefer canine to feline companionship but admit willingly that Schpatz was a most agreeable animal.

He had all the haughtiness one expects from a cat, but over the course of time he came to trust, and I think even to like me. On occasion when I was reading in the evening and drinking tea, he would leap so gingerly onto my lap below my upheld volume that I might not even notice him until his purr insinuated itself in my mind. I felt honoured in those moments and I made every attempt to stay still until he chose to leave, though his head became a weight on my bladder when he drifted to sleep.

A few days after my arrival, my host wisely decided to extend his stay in London for "at least the remainder of the summer." After the Anschluss in March, his Jewish heritage had made his habitation in Wolsenburg impossible and he was no longer permitted to draw his faculty salary. My own university in Canada had granted me a rather rare sabbatical and, as a gentile and a passivist I decided simply to carry on. My intended work in Wolsenburg was to be the study of the disputed Egger Codex, and particularly of the illuminations of which I had learned at the conference. This manuscript had only recently been found in the archives of the nearby castle and I was gleefully disquieted at the possibility that I might be the one to prove or disprove its veracity.

I prefer to spend a little while in a place rather than to pass through too quickly just to "see the sights". By staying in a city for a week or two, one begins to see not as a mere visitor, but as a resident. There must be time for trial and error. This bakery is best for bread but if you want a treat, try the Belgian down the lane who makes waffles with nuts and sugar. Soon one begins to know shortcuts and to feel the rhythms of the transit system, to anticipate crowds and to find what one needs. It is the difference between wondering "what would it be like to live here?" and knowing, "so this is how it is."

It was always my habit, when visiting a new city, to forsake transportation and go on foot as much as I could. In this way I developed a different relationship with a place and would go so far as to suggest that the place developed a sense of me. Cows and horses in the fields at a city's edge raise their heads, whereas anyone passing by in a car is ignored. Locals pay attention to someone on foot and one can quickly judge the relative tenor of welcome either by a passing nod of acquaintance or by the aversion of suspicious eyes. To walk in a city is to take full advantage of the sensual offerings of mass cohabitation — the smells, the pleasant scent of a tiny patisserie and the waft of a urine-soaked alleyway; the textures of paved walkways and cobbles and the immense relief of a turf parkway; not to mention the intricate images one might take in at a more relaxed pace. And of course, travelling à pied, as it were, also means moving in time in what I think of as a natural way. Before the advent of motor transport, time and distance were intimates. The measure of a particular destination might be expressed not with kilometers or some other, abstract gauge, but with time, as in: 'The very best apricots may be procured at the market in P—, two days west of here.' One might imagine the origins of the parental imperative to impatient children: 'Go run around the block a couple of times,' to have utilitarian origins in the measurement of time, so, for example, a soft boiled egg might be cooked perfectly in the time it took a child to run up to the cathedral steps and back.

Jay Ruzesky

I warmed to the city and took great pleasure in walking its narrow streets and in taking an afternoon coffee at an outdoor table from a little place in a square not far at all from the flat. Unless one requested something different, "a cup of coffee" in Wolsenburg meant a cup about the size of a heel of baguette filled with a rich portion of espresso, and topped with a substantial scoop of whipped cream. An excess of this particular pleasure was no doubt responsible for the slight increase in my weight those days despite the long walks.

The attractions tourists are drawn to can be spectacular, but often these exhibits are interesting only on the surface. Such is the case in Wolsenburg where by far the most popular destination for visitors is the tenth-century castle that overlooks the city from its perch high on Ziegenhirt hill. I was drawn to it because it housed the archives, yet it was quite some time before I bothered with the guided tour. The cathedral is a secondary stop, but holds inside it wonders that travellers would flock to if only they knew about it.

I passed by the Wolsenburg cathedral on the first day and stopped to admire the impressive stained glass rosette above the entrance way. I thought to myself that I should later like to see it from inside. I found the building very beautiful but knew too little about architecture to be able to date such a structure on sight or to identify many features besides buttresses and gothic arches. Many of my colleagues studied nothing but baroque flourishes on church columns. I had taken it upon myself to hold forth mainly on pre-Columbian brush strokes. What could be more fascinating, I wondered aloud to them, than the apocalyptic timetables of a vanished civilization? I contented myself with a glance up at the bell tower and spire, and made a mental note to return and have a look inside the cathedral the next day. In the morning it was raining heavily so I stayed late in bed. I have the kind of mind that likes to be occupied and though I am fond of losing myself in a good book, I began to look for distraction after an hour or so. A downpour is an excuse to stay put, so I lit the little gas fire to take off the chill, and passed the whole day that way, getting up occasionally to make a cup of tea or to eat some toast and then returning to Thomas Hardy's "Wessex" where love was being rejected and withheld again. Many people find Hardy depressing but it is a matter of perspective, I think. Certainly, poor Jude's dead children are nothing but tragic, but Hardy's bumbling rural characters are most comedic when they stop in at the pub on the way to a funeral just to "rest the weary soles, and well, yes, perhaps for a small glass."

It pleased me to manage to spend that much time reading, though because of the rain it was the third day of my visit before I got a look inside the cathedral and had my first glimpse of the Wolsenburg Clock.

An astronomical clock is much more than a timepiece. It articulates the passing of hours, naturally, but for the great, monumental astronomical clocks of Europe that is really a sideline. Such devices keep track of celestial motion and astronomical events; they measure the world and predict the future.

Oddly, there was little to be found in the Wolsenburg library on the subject of clocks, orreries, and planetariums. In a gesture which I see now was an acknowledgement of my intention to remain longer, I had my university send me two volumes from their holdings. These remain in my possession to this day and are a source of discomfort for me. I have never been a book thief and to ease my conscience, I have included a provision in my will to have them returned upon my demise.

Through this reading I discovered that an early working model of the universe was built by Archimedes in the third century BC, although we know about it only through references in literature. In medieval China, celestial wheels were rotated by the use of water gears, as were similar displays in the Islamic world of the Middle East.

By the end of the fourteenth century, most European towns large enough to support significant trade and a cathedral had a central clock of some sort. These were fantastic devices with detailed automata and dancing statues that came out of doors and hidden compartments to strike chimes on the hour or even on the quarter hour. There were massive, richly-painted dials that showed the phases of the moon and indicated important feast days. Such clocks provided locals, particularly merchants, with a standard time service they could depend upon. By displaying the moon cycle, these clocks allowed parishioners to plan the best times for long night journeys by moonlight. For the most part, medieval monumental clocks were constructed on and in churches because their other function was to remind parishioners of God's perfect order in the universe and of their role in that order: sowing, tending, harvesting, and reaping so that God's plan for each of them could be revealed 'in good time'.

Of course, thirteenth century astronomers recognized that the universe was not nearly so well ordered as the clergy would have liked. In fact, 'corrections' to the calendar were introduced by Julius Caesar on the advice of Sosigenes, his loyal astronomer. Caesar added leap years to try to correct the system but Caesar's method was not entirely accurate either. By the end of the sixteenth century, the civil year began about ten days too early so Pope Gregory made further changes. Some countries, Greece, Russia and Turkey for example, refused to accept the new system until the twentieth century. In the Gregorian calendar the Julian leap-year rule is altered so that years divisible by one hundred are not leap years unless they are also divisible by four hundred in which case the leap year is maintained. Gregory also decreed that October 4th, 1582 should be followed immediately by October 15th, 1582 thus correcting the calendar but robbing thousands of civilians of their birthdays that year. Eleven days disappeared like magic and there were protests by labourers who feared the loss of ten days' wages.

I entered the building the way I always do a church — by ducking in uncertainly. As an unbeliever, I never know when there might be some ritual in progress that I would be intruding upon. I have an image in mind of a worshiper kneeling, just about to receive forgiveness or redemption or a great epiphany, when suddenly their reverie is disrupted by the creak of a door and my peering form breaking the spell forever. St. Thomas Aquinas is said to have levitated at prayer early one morning and I wouldn't like to think I was responsible for bringing an ecstatic worshiper down to earth with a crash. Fortunately, there seemed to be no one at all inside the main building.

The structure is impressive: two dozen massive pillars run down the aisle from the entrance toward the altar holding up an astonishingly high, arched stone ceiling. Rich stained glass windows line the hall and small, coloured clerestory windows at the apex of wall and ceiling allow solid beams of light to be directed into the pews like spotlights. There is the smell of age-old incense and a kind of musk that seems to rise up out of the polished floor that is of some sort of dark green, almost black stone. It gleams with all the colours the windows drape over it. Near the altar is a bank of votive candles that seem so numerous one might imagine that the flames represent the glimmering souls of every person in the city. To the left of the altar is an elaborate pulpit, carved from oak, cherry, and rosewood, and to the right is the clock — at any given moment suggestive of a veritable colony of movement and activity.

I approached it with curiosity. Truly, I had never seen a clock inside a cathedral and my initial thought was to wonder what the thing was doing there. Was it simply being stored out of the rain while its proper resting place was being made ready? As I drew nearer I heard a click and a purr. My attention was drawn up to the top of a tall wooden turret on the left (which I learned housed the drive weights for the machine). This part of the structure was perhaps forty-five or fifty feet high and was surmounted by a rooster which looked, from my vantage point, in every way like a live creature. The cock flapped its wings as if preparing to sound out, but settled itself just as a door beneath it opened. Out of the door crawled a child, or perhaps a cherub, but certainly an infantile one, which waddled around to the middle of the turret and lifted a trumpet which it swung one time against a central bell to announce the passing of the first quarter of the hour before continuing along its circular pathway and disappearing behind another little door on the other side of the bell, its knees churning like pedals on a bicycle.

It was a magical moment and I was still absorbing it when a figure approached me from the direction of the vestibule to the side and slightly behind the clock. At first, I thought he might be another part of the display, but as he drew nearer, I saw he was not at all mechanical.

As a way of introducing himself, he announced that there was no finer clock in all of Europe. He spoke in English and had an accent that squashed the 'th's over his lower lip and pushed his 'r's up to the roof of his mouth. I have no idea how he knew to speak to me in English. I'm assuming he guessed.

I managed to say that I had never seen anything quite like it and he replied quickly that the simple reason was that there was not anything like it and there never would be. I smiled and nodded agreement and he stepped forward a pace and held out his hand, giving his name as Josias Stimmler, the keeper of the clock.

I am of the school of thought that says a handshake is an offering and not a competition. Some men seem to feel more masculine if they can inflict a little pain with a tight squeeze. In my opinion, a handshake is an invitation of trust to allow another into one's close personal space. The actual handshake ought to be not much more than a socially conditioned touch, and it is the breaking of the spatial boundaries that is the real test of the gesture.

However, as I accepted Stimmler's hand, there was a loud crunch and grinding of bone. I drew back my hand as though from a flame, terrified that I had done him some injury but he told me not to worry; that the noise was the result of some "condition" as he referred to it. He had not been to see a doctor about it, nor was he particularly concerned. He claimed that all of his bones were similarly affected and that it caused him no pain. In fact, he said that he forgot all about it when he was on his own and as a kind of illustration, he balled up his fists and shifted his shoulders to produce a horrible series of popping sounds like the noise of someone walking across a fire built of small twigs.

In the time I spent with Stimmler, looking into the workings of the clock and listening to his stories of its origins, I was often unnerved by this affliction of his and never did become accustomed to it.

The tale of the Wolsenburg clock is itself a fabulous construction. It is fair to say that the clock was built over a period of 625 years. The idea of it, the marvellous seed that has blossomed into this glorious garden of technology, was planted beyond all reason in 1378 as the construction of the cathedral itself was nearing completion. It was not enough, it seems, for the chieftains of the town to have built a gargantuan temple at the centre of the people's lives; they wanted to install within it a heart to bring the structure to life, a kind of motor for God.

The glory of the Wolsenburg clock is in its wood, copper, carved stone, and other elements not easily identified, and in those who put the components there. It is in the dials that indicate sidereal time, the phases of the moon, the motion of the known planets and the sun, and of a range of stars including the entire Milky Way. It is in the statue of Mercury that points to the current date on a dial geared to be accurate even during leap years, and in the cock with a bellows in its throat which emerges to crow during the afternoon procession of the apostles. These are but some of its charms.

It is Stimmler of the crackling bones that I have to thank for opening to me a world of wonders I had no hint of before, and him I can blame for my new found belief in the divine.

Naturally, the clock is also about the people who carved its cabinets, shaped the gilded moldings, painted the face boards. To look at the clock is to see into the lives of these people. It is like the experience I once had when I walked along the banks of the Seine in Paris. I realized that each of the stones had been *put* there with purpose. In fact, the whole of the city of Paris, every brick, every cobblestone, was set in place by a builder, and each builder had a life and so a story.

I have a passion for my chosen work with the minutiae of history. I know that it is vital that I do everything I can to work for precision as a researcher and to follow names and dates to their ends before choosing another avenue of exploration. Accuracy matters. And yet these are not mere facts and figures to me. A name is not an idea; it is a living being. A date is not a marker of the past, it is a day in which the sun shone, or the rain fell, or the snow piled up on the church steps. The work of delving into detail as I do, gives me a glimpse into the very character of the people who occupy those moments. Would that I could write like Thomas Hardy and represent those people with all of their human strengths and human flaws, their greed and their humour. I wish I could in some way make them real again. I would like to write their story in a way that would make even my old colleagues pay attention, in a way that would help others know what the clock has taught me.

The Medieval Clock — 1378

Wildrik Kiening's assistant, Leon, brought him the eyeballs of an ox in a wooden bowl ripe with viscous fluid and Wildrik could scarcely stop drooling at the sight of them, his salivary glands nudged toward excitement as much by the thought of handling the staring ocular globes as by the oxtail soup that was already simmering near the fire. He lifted one from the bowl and let it rest in his palm a moment. It jiggled slightly, the way a bladder filled with liquid will, and its iris gauged his intent with apparent unconcern until he withdrew his cutting tool from a leather apron of instruments that was spread before him on the table. He sliced away the back of the eyeball and propped what was left on a stand at the centre of his worktable, and then rested a white goose egg behind it. He placed a portrait of a peasant maiden in a field before the eye and directed his lamp toward it.

"Look Leon! Look at the egg!" An image of the portrait, reversed and inverted appeared on the shell.

"What am I looking at?"

"The egg, you dunderwit! Look at the egg! Can you not see the painting there?"

"Yes. And so?"

"And so, what . . . what does it look like?"

"I don't know, sir. It looks, um, fuzzy."

"Fuzzy? This is why I have a reputation and you are merely an errand boy."

"An errand boy perhaps, and also your own personal jester. I know more than one around here thinks you have a bit of a wobble between your earwax, and I think you should be more grateful for my services. I may not be serving up your bovid spilth much longer if you don't pay me a little recompense for my troubles some day soon. Sir."

Wildrik lowered himself to the edge of the table so that his own eye was staring at the eye of the ox. "Look here Leon. The image is reproduced exactly. All of the detail has been conveyed through the lens but it has been turned on its head. I can rotate the egg, you see, and the image remains inverted. How could this be so? Does the ox see the world upside down? Does it live in constant fear of falling up?"

"It looked worried to me but then again I'm the one who walloped it in the skull with my mallet. It had some cause for concern."

Wildrik stood. "Do you know Psalm 94, Leon?"

"Remind me."

"*Does he who formed the eye not see?*"

"And what does that have to do with the eyeball I plucked out of the ox?"

"This eye on my table is a world of infinite art. It is this, the reception of light through the eye that distinguishes the living from the dead. The image that passes through the eye to rest on the egg is a beautiful small world and when we look at it, that small world is again projected — a small world within a small world within a small world — through our own eyes and into our minds. Without the eye, the beauties of nature would be meaningless. It is because God gave us eyes that we can see."

"Well, if that is so, how do we manage to see right side up? How can I be sure that I am not standing on my head?"

"I don't know, Leon. I don't know."

The door to Wildrik's chamber blew open as though forced by a brawny gust, and two of the Bishop of Wolsenburg's footmen scrambled to attention on either side of the entrance, followed by the prelate himself, his white robes flowing behind him.

"Always with the grand entrance," Leon whispered in Wildrik's ear.

Wildrik was still holding the blade and dropped it expertly so it landed point down on the table and stuck quivering there dangerously close to Leon's breeches. Leon was forced to jump back and snap to attention as Wildrik moved forward to kiss the ring on the bishop's outstretched hand. "Your Excellency," he said, "you do me honour with your visit."

"It can't be helped," boomed the bishop. He was a great lout of a man, fat with the charity of parishioners and rank with the ooze of imported wine from his pores. He called for a chair and Wildrik snapped his fingers to summon Leon to bring forward a seat. The bishop sat. He wiped his sleeve across his bulbous, leaking nose, drew forth a quantity of phlegm with a guttural roar and swallowed it down.

"May I offer you some mead, Excellency?" Wildrik asked.

"No," said the bishop.

"Ale? Bread with a pat of butter? Cakes? A haunch of mutton?" Leon asked.

"I want you to build me an orologium."

"A what?" Leon said.

"A clock," said Wildrik.

"Not just a clock," said the bishop, "I have been on a visit to Strasbourg and seen in the cathedral there a machine that was a wonder to behold. It was the firmament in miniature made in copper and gold and it foretold the movements of the planets in the heavenly spheres. With this device, the citizens of Strasbourg may harmonize their activities, plan the sowing of crops and their harvest. I want Wolsenburg to have one even more splendid."

"What's a clock?" asked Leon, but Wildrik stifled him with a damning look and an elbow to the mid-section.

Wildrik's white still body was laid out on his bed. He was naked; a sheet covered him. His wife, Albruna, approached him and peeled back the shroud. She looked at his face, peaceful as though in sleep, and she folded the sheet further so his mid-section was exposed. She climbed on the bed beside him and kneeled there a while, then licked the end of her thumb and made the sign of the cross — one gesture down his forehead to his nose and a horizontal line across his brow. Then with her whole flat palm, she made the same sign on his chest beginning with the horizontal this time, and then slowly pulling her hand from his neck down the length of him. When her fingers touched below his navel, he sat bolt upright and she screamed, then laughed as he pulled her down to cover him.

"It's freezing in here," he said. "A man could die of cold and last for months before the stink of death caught up with him."

"That's because you spend all our money on bits of glass and paper and things we can't eat or use to warm the house," Albruna said.

"There was the ox," he said.

"True," she said, "it did have a most practical application."

"Can't burn it for heat though, as you say."

"I'll have to warm you up then, won't I?" she said, straddling him and sitting up. Her gown bunched around her hips and he held his hands there, below her waist, then slid them slowly up the front of her body. She let him. She watched his face as he moved his hands up her sides until his palms could sense the edges of her breasts, and kept her gaze as he moved his hands around forward so he held her like taps he wanted to turn. His thumbs circled around, then over her nipples, sending little vibrations back toward her centre. She arched a little and she saw his brow furrow. His hands stopped moving. He sat up and pushed her back slightly, reached down to the edges of the gown and pulled it over her head unceremoniously so he could see her naked form. It *was* cold. She shivered. He reached out for her breasts again, slowly turning his hand around the left one and lifting a little while studying the texture of her flesh.

Jay Ruzesky

"It's quite interesting, from a design point of view," he said. "Its placement at the front of the body is a little baffling to me. I might have tucked them away somewhere, under the arms perhaps, where they might be more protected. And have them fold up or empty out when not in use."

"You wish my breasts were under my armpits?"

"No, no. Not yours specifically, but if I was God I might have made some changes."

"Do you think that would be comfortable? Consider what a rash might do and the changes of temperature under there. What about when they are 'in use' as you say. I can't imagine you would be very popular with mothers who had to walk around like ducks as long as their children were nursing."

"I see what you mean, but what about the male then?" he said, looking down at his own chest. "Why bother with nipples as all? What point is there in my having them?"

Albruna leaned forward and took one of his nipples in her mouth, then sucked as hard as she could.

"Oh," Wildrik said, "I see. Yes, absolutely."

She pushed him back down on the bed and rose above him again. "Is there any other part of my anatomy you would like to muse upon?" she asked him, reaching for him between her legs.

There was writhing and bouncing, turning back and forth, some twisting, considerable rubbing, greatly increased heart rates, a certain blotchy reddening across the entire surface area of milky skin on her part, and a sort of overall increase in temperature for him; there were sounds of exertion and pleasure, and other liquidy noises more difficult to identify, and a rather sudden cessation of it all ending in a mutual collapse and the sound of sprinters after a race.

"Lord God," Albruna said, rolling onto her back beside Wildrik and pulling the sheet and blanket to cover them both.

"Well, no," he said, "it was just me . . . "

"Blasphemy," she slapped him with a backhand.

"But if I was God I might be inclined to make some changes to that process too."

"You wouldn't dare," she said.

"No, right, I wouldn't," he said.

"Wildrik, sometimes it is not so useful to ask questions. Sometimes, *sometimes*, it is not even so good to think so much."

Wisely, he said nothing in response and they both looked up at the ceiling for a while not moving.

"I think you're getting the hang of it," she said.

"I cheated," he said.

"What do you mean you cheated?"

"I was thinking about other things instead."

"Like what?"

"Clocks," he said.

"Clocks?"

"Clocks."

"All right then, I give up. What's a clock?"

The orologium was also to be the reliquary for the remains of St. Peter which the bishop had secured for the cathedral at no small cost and with considerable effort. In the end, because of the highly sacred nature of Peter's remains and their control by the Vatican, all the bishop was able to obtain was St. Peter's middle finger, and because of a rather questionable bargain he struck with the cardinal who had managed to provide the relic after several weeks' prayer and fasting, all involved thought it best that the cathedral not be named after the Apostle.

At any rate, part of Wildrik's project was to devise a chamber within the clock for Peter's remains.

"How can we be sure that's his *finger*?" Leon wanted to know.

While the Bishop of Wolsenburg milked everyone in the parish for funds to build the clock, Wildrik Kiening traveled to Strasbourg to look at the one there. As he approached it for the first time, he began to salivate as he always did when his mind was moving more quickly than he could keep up with.

The astronomical clock in the Strasbourg cathedral was fifty-five feet high and though dwarfed by the full height of the cathedral itself, was awesome to behold. At the very top point of the tower was a cockerel made of iron, copper, silk, and wood. Wildrik happened to arrive just before noon, so was there when the gilded creature flapped its wings, spread its feathers, opened its beak, put out its tongue, and crowed.

"Ingenious," he said. The crow contained a bellows and a reed and its wings were operated by a series of wires.

Also at noon, in the top section, three automated kings bowed before statuettes of the Virgin and Christ while a small carillon played a tune. In the middle section there was a large astrolabe-dial, perhaps twelve feet across, and below that a circular wooden dial which served as a calendar pointing out the day of the week, the date, year, and indicating feast days. At the bottom, the figure of a man showed the relationship between the signs of the zodiac and the human body.

Wildrik had been given permission to study the clock's works, but he spent his first day in Strasbourg simply staring at the machine and salivating.

Albruna accompanied Wildrik to Strasbourg. It was seven days by carriage. On the way back home, she reclined into the velvet corner of the conveyance and Wildrik leaned his head on his wife's chest. The motion of the wheels on the rutted road rocked them both toward sleep. Though he was resting his body, Wildrik's mind was racing. Already he was beginning to envision the completed clock.

Despite his excess of all four bodily humours, the bishop was nothing if not generous with money. He granted Wildrik a substantial advance and was reasonable about his demands. Wildrik was given four years to complete his work.

The clock would be set into motion at the celebration to commemorate the completion of the cathedral. Generations of tradesmen had worked until old age and their kin were just now putting the finishing touches on the structure.

In four years, the bell tower would ignite with sound and the entire parish would rejoice. They would enter the cathedral for the first time, and become breathless at the interior height. The columns would seem to be holding up not a mere ceiling, but the very heavens, carved of stone and arched into place.

And in the midst of that feeling of expansiveness, of the overwhelming magnitude of their universe, something else would catch the eye of these innocent worshipers. A glint of gold, a subtle movement. *What's this?* they would think, the orologium capturing their attention and drawing them near. *What beauty, what elegance!* they would cock their heads, study the dials, admire the figures. It would occur to them suddenly, and would nearly knock them off their feet: what they were looking at would be nothing less than a representation of their universe in miniature, and they, standing before it, had been placed in the position of God, standing back to watch the majesty of the cosmos unfolding. It would be a gift beyond imagining and it was Wildrik who would give it to them.

The carriage rocked. Wildrik lost himself in his reverie. Albruna's chest rose and fell with her breathing, and his ear, pressed against the chamber of her being, registered her heart counting time. Boom, boom, boom. The wheel jarred sending them both off their seat. Albruna roused herself from her dreams and felt moisture at the front of her dress.

"Do sit up, dearest," she said.

Albruna carried a candle and two cups of warmed mead into Wildrik's workshop in the middle of the night. She found him asleep on his table amid a great sea of numbers. For three months he had been drawing plans and making calculations. Some days now he spoke only in figures and she gauged his desires by his body language rather than by anything he said.

She would ask if he was hungry and he might answer: "... the transmission rod will need to carry two pinions where one drives wheel 116 of the sun plate at one turn in $116/19 \times 4h = 24h$."

In response she would bring him a bowl of pottage and some wine, or just wine, or just pottage. She knew him so well that she could discern what his body needed, even if he wasn't able to figure that out.

She found his shoulder under a scroll of paper and gently shifted the sheet onto the table before touching his slack muscle. He roused himself and looked around the room in a daze, smacking his lips and chewing the air. As he lifted from his sleep, another pile of paper in the corner of the room burst upward as Leon snorted and jumped off the stool he had been drowsing on.

"You are both working too hard," she said. "You can't keep this up."

"Train 17 will be fixed so 17, 54 + 15, 33 rotates the hands of the nodes dial once in 6.6 years," Wildrik said.

"Ditto," Leon said.

Wildrik's face wore a tattoo of gears from the design of the zodiac plate where he had slept on wet ink.

"You must come to bed," Albruna reached for his arm.

Leon stepped forward and offered his own wing when he saw Wildrik resisting.

"*You* must *go* to bed," she told him.

"Why do you always pick him?" Leon shouted, and he stormed out of the room in mock disgust.

Wildrik was back to full consciousness. His eyes were glowing and he was salivating wildly.

"Wildrik, is something wrong with you?"

"Not with me," he said, "there is something wrong with God."

It happens that the cardinal will be here in a few days," said the bishop. "Perhaps he will be able to make some sense of you. I have no idea what you are talking about. Let me warn you though, if you cause anyone, particularly, but not exclusively, His Eminence and His Holiness to look unfavourably upon me or my cathedral or my orologium, I shall have you killed in the most unpleasant manner I can imagine."

"Certainly, your Excellency," said Wildrik. He paused, "What do you mean *your* orologium?"

The cardinal was a man of science. Wildrik was admitted to see him as he was taking his lunch.

"Your Eminence. Thank you for seeing me," Wildrik said. "If I might be permitted to explain what my calculations have revealed . . . "

"Sit down, sit down," the cardinal said. He motioned for a plate and drinking glass for Wildrik, and delicately dabbed some quail juice from the side of his mouth with his napkin. "The wine is from Rome; drink, eat."

"Thank you, Your Eminence." He quaffed a quantity of wine and was momentarily distracted by its depth. "It is very fine indeed. Thank you."

The cardinal had a thin face and light blue eyes that studied his guest as Wildrik popped a roasted lark in his mouth and crunched the bones, then washed it down with wine. Taken with the wealth of offerings before him, Wildrik forgot himself and gorged on some cheese and the cardinal continued to gaze and sat back in his chair. He pushed away his own full plate and one of the servants behind him rushed forward to remove it. "Now," he said, "the bishop tells me you have run into a problem with the stars. Already I think you fortunate since most people's trouble has to do with getting enough to eat."

Wildrik lifted his face from the cheese and felt the full effect of the cardinal's stare. He slowly righted himself from his hunch over the food and brushed his hands gently over the plate and tried to swallow. "I too think myself most fortunate, Eminence. God has provided me with a charmed existence."

"But . . . " the thin face relaxed and there was a hint of amusement in the blue eyes which put Wildrik at ease.

Jay Ruzesky

"It is the stars, Eminence. The calendar. The year. Time. We have it all wrong."

The cardinal clasped his hands together before him and rested his chin on his mingled knuckles. "Explain," he said, "and go slowly. I do not understand things quickly." He closed his eyes and leaned forward with his head slightly cocked, as if preparing to hear Wildrik's confession.

"The orologium will be a magnificent device. I have such plans, Excellency. It will make the irreverent devout. I want the parishioners to gaze upon my clock and see before them the perfection of a universe designed by God. I want them to know that their lives are ordered and predictable, that they are part of a great symphony of the movement of the planetary spheres, and that just as the moon has reason to revolve around the earth, they have reason to live their lives."

"A worthy ambition. Go on," the cardinal nodded.

"My calculations have revealed an error that casts aspersions on all of my work. As you know, the calendar was created by Caesar to standardize the measurement of time. His astronomers computed a year to be 365 and 1/4 days long. It is their reasoning that has given us the leap year every four years, the purpose of which is to accommodate this extra quarter of a day, and with these leap days, we maintain the illusion of an ordered cosmos."

"You say it is an illusion?"

"Caesar's astronomers, Your Eminence, were wrong."

"By how much?"

"Eleven minutes and fourteen seconds."

"Well, that's not much. Why trifle about it?"

"It has been a century and a half since the Julian calendar was instituted. The inconsistency grows by the year and if it remains uncorrected, the vernal equinox will be in mid-winter. Imagine the chaos, Eminence. Imagine the doubt of the people. What kind of a world will it be? If we can't count on time, what can we count on? Already, the gap is growing."

"What do you mean?"

"At present, the equinoxes occur about eight and a half days early."

"Are you sure?" the cardinal asked.

"Eminence, I would stake my life on it. I have done so with the bishop. I tell you this not to shake the faith of the people, but in order that you might help me maintain it by giving them a clock that will be accurate. I am a scientist and a man of reason, and I am also a man of faith. As are you Your Eminence. I have heard of astronomers who have begun to doubt that the sun moves around the earth. As passengers on a ship in motion might perceive a still and distant ship to be moving, so it may be with the sun, they say. Perhaps it is the earth that is in motion, revolving around the sun."

"Hah! If that were true, then what about Aristotle's proof that if the earth were in motion, we would feel the wind from the movement just, as you say, passengers on a moving ship feel a wind even on a calm day?" asked the cardinal.

"I agree, I agree. But how then do I reconcile my problem with the hours in a year? I believe my calculations to be true, but I cannot explain to you why they are true, and if summer feast days begin to be celebrated in winter and spring happens in autumn, the people may look for answers neither you nor I will find comfortable."

The cardinal shook his head, hoping that he would be able to keep it when he explained the problem to the pope.

It took the cardinal three months to travel to the Holy See and come back with an answer. In the meantime, Wildrik was able to continue with his plans. He would have to hold off on some of the more the precise calculations for leap years in the calendar dial, but the rest of the ratios were accurate, and he could begin to order materials and figure the mechanics of other moving parts, like the automata and the bells. Whether the pope took his advice or not, the clock would keep perfect time. The question was, would it keep perfect time the Vatican's way, or God's?

The clock would be sixty feet high. At the top, a cockerel similar to the one in Strasbourg, and below it a chamber to hold a figure of Peter and of Jesus. At the beginning and the end of the day, Peter and Jesus would emerge from separate doors in the chamber; the cock would crow three times and Peter would turn his back on Christ. Christ would open his arms then both figures would withdraw back into the chamber and the drama would repeat at the end of the day. Under the automata, Wildrik would build a chamber for the carillon with open spaces and pillars so parishioners could see the bells from below and it would appear as though they were played by spirits.

Below the carillon, the astrolabe. Wildrik would make it monumental — fifteen feet around. The rete would be just half that. The sun hand would feature a solid gold orb to arc through the figures of the zodiac. Wildrik had devised a clever system of dials so that the moon hand would shift over a dial painted half black and half white, and as the dial rotated, its glass circle would reveal different ratios and within would mimic the phases of the moon. The day section would be painted white and azure blue and divided into twelve equal partitions. Another innovation would be pointers for the five planets, for which Wildrik had commissioned an artist to design a serpent with five heads, the points of which would writhe independently to follow the movement of the celestial bodies.

Under the astrolabe would be the calendar-dial, slightly smaller than the astrolabe — just ten feet around. The date ring would be divided into 366 intervals, each showing the day of the month, the Dominical letter, and the name of the Saint commemorated. On St. Peter's day, the cockerel would crow at noon, as well as in the morning and evening. All the while the carillon would play a hymn unique to that day.

The passage of each day would be made instantaneously at midnight, and Wildrik had after vast calculations devised a system whereby in common years the first of March followed February twenty-eighth, but on leap years a disk with a numeral nine painted on it would drop down and cover the eight at the same time suspending the works of the movement of the larger dial for one day. Another plate associated with the calendar dial would pass through one division a year and would display the year and the time of the spring equinox. In a separate column to the left of the major works, a train of animals, one to represent each day of the week, would make their slow procession. The bells would ring out the hour and the quarter hour and would be engaged to perform specific pieces of music on particular feast days.

Wildrik had been planning so long that he could now envision the entire structure, could imagine where the pointers would be at any time of the day, and could hear the chimes of the bells in his mind. The dream of the clock was true. Now all he had to do was build it.

He hadn't yet resolved what to do with St. Peter's finger.

He didn't want to wake Albruna, and since her head was resting on his chest, he had no choice but to stay still. Full of thought, he looked about the room. His mouth began to water and he shifted just slightly.

"Your heart is a clock," Albruna said this without moving. "I can hear you ticking."

"Let me try," he said, and he pushed her over and listened to her chest. Her heart beat a steady rhythm. "Ah, you astonish me. Your heart is beating precisely in seconds. It is exactly right. I could regulate my orologium with you."

"I think it does not always beat so consistently. For instance, it quickens with exertion."

"How do you know?"

"Well, I don't know. I merely suppose. Perhaps an experiment is in order."

"I do love an experiment," he said.

I have Pope Gregory's ear," the cardinal said. "I explained your calculations to him and he was most interested and most distressed. I also suggested your compromise — the correction of the calendar and the extension of the Julian leap year rule so that years divisible by one hundred but not four hundred should be counted as common years."

"And what did he say, Eminence?" Wildrik asked.

"I think the mathematics escaped him, but the threat of panic and riots made sense, and the astronomers at the Vatican concurred with your work. In fact, they said you must be rather a brilliant man."

"Excellent then. What is to be done?"

"Nothing."

"Why not!"

The cardinal gave him a warning glance.

"Pardon me Eminence. I mean, did he give a reason?"

"He didn't have much of a chance. He died. I have his ear, but the rest of him is still in Rome."

"Forgive my impertinence Eminence, but did you speak to the new Pontiff about my suggestion?"

"I am afraid that Urban VI is not so . . . reasonable as his predecessor. I don't believe I will be able to convince him. I was not in favour of his election and I need to keep my distance for a time. You simply have to make your clock work according to the calendar as it is. And you would do well to keep your calculations to yourself. The consequences of the spread of your ideas might be disastrous. Particularly for you."

"I understand Eminence."

"The good news is, I brought you a cask of wine."

Leon supervised the delivery of oak planking and had it moved into the cathedral. Some parts of the orologium would be constructed elsewhere to be assembled and fitted into place later; very fine detail work was done at Wildrik's workshop or in the studios and sheds of smiths and artisans. Other, larger aspects of the clock needed to be manufactured at the site. It was Leon's responsibility to oversee the first stage of construction within the cathedral.

Already he had confrontations with masons at work there. In order to secure the clock, it was necessary to carve holes in the inside wall of the south transept which were to be filled with lead anchor-plugs.

"You want us to desecrate work that has taken seventy-five years to complete? My grandfather helped lay that stone and you want me to put a hole in it?" one of the masons said. A small crowd of workers was gathering around.

Leon could see it was going to be a long day. "Gentlemen," he said, "you honour your forefathers by continuing their work. I stand here in awe of your accomplishment. It is not only the scale of the cathedral that impresses, but the care in the minute details: the carvings and stone joinery."

"And you want us to knock holes in it?" the mason asked him.

"Look. I am one of you. People are going to come in here two years hence and the building itself will make them think about God. You and I know that it is with God's help that you have made this edifice; God has made the stone strong; God has kept the ceiling from collapsing. How many have died in the construction? None. Not one soul has been lost. That is God's will and nothing else."

"What do you mean not one soul?" one of the other masons shouted. "Many men have spent their years working with the stones in this building and are not alive to see it finished."

"Not to mention all those whose backs have been permanently warped by work," the first mason protested.

"Or the people who were taxed to starvation to pay for all of this," the other man said.

"To put a hole in this wall is to drive a stake into the flesh of all those who laboured here. It's an abomination," the first mason said.

"My friends!" Leon stepped between them. "Please, please. God's will has made the cathedral strong, God's will impresses us all. But *your* hands shifted these stones. Every day for seventy-five years you, and your fathers, and your father's fathers went home at the end of the day with aching muscles and strained eyes, dust in your hair, and grit in your lungs. Why? Why may I ask have you worked so?"

"To get paid," the second mason said.

"Well, yes, naturally," said Leon. "But, also because it is God's will; part of God's divine plan. The orologium to be constructed here will be nothing short of a tribute to the work you have been doing. Each quarter hour, the chimes will ring out to remind us of the entire lives that went by in the building of this monumental palace of God and of our own mortality; how our short lives are best lived by watching the unfolding of the spectacular design of the universe."

There was silence as the workers took in Leon's speech.

"Here's my hammer then," the first mason said. "I'm still not doing it."

With a sigh, Leon took the tool, approached the mark on the wall and tapped.

On the feast of St. Peter's Chains, August 1st, 1380, Wildrik played chess with the bishop in the city square. The bishop was a more wily player than most of his rivals first imagined, but Wildrik discerned his strategy quickly. The bishop's vulnerability, quite naturally, was that he was overly protective with his bishops and as a result, would take greater risks with the other pieces. Wildrik, with astute diplomacy, played his own kind of game, attempting to keep the bishop's bishops in constant threat without actually capturing them. In the end, he let the bishop win more often than lose and that helped him get the things he needed — more gold for the ornamentation of the clock, or an increase in provisions for the small army of gun founders and smiths he now had forging gears, wheels and plates for him.

Wildrik thought, *he is like a dog. Throw him a scanty bone now and again and he will give me what I want.*

Some children ran by engaged at hoodman's blind, and a crowd was gathered at the top of the square betting on cockfights. Another group clustered around a stall playing dice.

"The work goes well, I see," said the bishop.

"The main structure is complete," Wildrik said. "The rest of the effort is in the details. There is much finishing to do and once I have all the works in place, it will be a delicate task to tune them all correctly."

"Will it be ready in time?" the bishop asked.

"I have no doubt, Excellency," Wildrik said.

"One year from today then, we shall consecrate the great cathedral of Wolsenburg by setting into motion the wheels of the greatest orologium ever made."

"We will indeed, Excellency," Wildrik hoisted his mug of ale and took a drink.

The cockfights had ended and a rather large contingent of peasants was passing by the spot where the bishop and Wildrik were seated. They were glancing at the two men and whispering as they went by.

The bishop hated gossip. He stood up quickly, bumping his paunch against the table and upsetting pieces on the board of the game he had been losing. "Here now, stop where you are," he barked at the passersby. "Tell me why you whisper as you pass. What rumours are you spreading?"

The peasants looked horrified.

The bishop took a step and pulled a young woman forward by her earlobe, which just barely protruded from beneath her tight cap. "Tell me what they say," the bishop yelled.

Rather than cowering before him, the woman pulled the bishop's hand from her ear and stood up straight. "They merely sing your praises, Excellency" she said boldly, bowing her head.

The bishop was caught off guard by her impertinence. "Nonsense," he said. "You may speak plainly. Tell me what they say."

"I think you will not be pleased," she said.

"I don't expect to be," the bishop said. "Go on."

"All right then," she said, "they say they do not mind so much that you grow fat on their labours, but that it is a great shame that they must ruin their backs so that you might build a toy in the cathedral."Wildrik leapt to his feet, sending the game flying so that the peasants had to duck airborne chess pieces. "A toy!" he gasped. "A *toy*!" He raised his hand to strike her but stopped himself in mid-swing just before his open hand could hit her face. The woman had not flinched. She was staring at him with her chin upraised, prepared to take the blow full on. The rest of the crowd stood motionless, watching the grim tableau.

Albruna had come upon the scene as the peasants were dispersing. Wildrik was in a knot of anxiety. She removed him from the square and made him stand in a doorway while she filled her basket in the tavern with bread and a crock of ale and then she guided him out of the city. Simply walking helped to put him at ease. They strode up a stone road without speaking until the road became a track, and the track became a trail, and they climbed a hill in a field where Albruna spread a linen and laid out the food and drink. They drank ale and ate, and eventually talked, and the sun dropped behind a distant rise and twilight deepened the sky in which a slight crescent moon hung low on the horizon. They could see the city and in its centre, the massive spire of the nearly finished cathedral.

"It is only natural that they should be suspicious. Until the orologium is finished and they can marvel at its wonders, you cannot expect the people to understand. I barely make sense of you myself most days," Albruna said.

"Yes, I know, but she called it a toy! It is not a mere plaything, Albruna."

"Of course not."

"There is something more as well," he said.

"What?"

"It is *not* a toy I am building. I have never been so driven to complete anything in my life. I have never been so possessed by any project and I believe . . . I believe it is God's will that I make this clock as an illustration of the glories of His world . . . "

"Yes, yes, of course; you cannot let ignorance deter you."

"The problem comes when I think of those who protest. The people who pay for the gold leaf are the same people who cannot get enough to eat in winter. The problem is, I wonder if, in some ways, they may be right."

"Wildrik, you are as complicated as the orologium itself. Have I ever told you that?" Albruna said.

"Indeed," he said.

They were silent a while and all the stars came out. There was a streak of light against the darkness and then another. They watched as every few minutes a star seemed to fall from the sky.

"Wildrik," Albruna said, "what is happening to the stars?"

"No need to fear, Albruna. Such phenomena have been witnessed many, many times before, and as astronomy tells us, even such storms as these do not reduce the numbers of stars.

"What are we to make of this then?"

"I cannot say exactly, but I do not think it is a good sign," he said.

Later, the bishop commented on the exchange with the young woman: "Throw them a bone now and again and they will do as we please," he said. "In the end, their actions matter more to me than their opinions."

The winter was particularly cold. Wildrik's fingers nearly froze as he tinkered with the works of the orologium. Gears with imperfections needed to be recast, and in some cases, the smiths had failed to follow his directions exactly, not realizing that the smallest difference in the size of a wheel or the number of teeth on a gear would throw the whole device off.

At work one morning, he was approached by a woodsmith who had been doing finishing work on the pulpit.

"Excuse me, sir."

"Yes, what is it?" Wildrik had his head wedged into the space between the wall and the clock.

"They say you are a healer sir," the man said.

Frustrated, Wildrik withdrew from the orologium and wiped his hands on his cape as he stood back to study the man. "I know something of the planetary alignments and the way the constellations influence the humours and the spirits. What is your trouble?"

"It's not me. It's my son. I wonder if you could come."

Wildrik could see he was desperate so he let the man lead the way.

From the outside, the carpenter's house appeared similar to Wildrik's. It was made of the same stone, but was only one level. Inside though, it was dramatically different. Where Wildrik and Albruna lived in five different rooms with tapestries on the walls to stifle drafts and wood in the hearths for heat, the carpenter and his family lived together in one small room, with earth on the floors and no heat. They could barely afford fuel to cook with.

It was no warmer inside than out. The carpenter's son was laid on a cot and was covered with every warm blanket and piece of clothing the family could spare.

Wildrik called for candles so he could study the boy, and though their supply of wax was limited, they lit five sticks and held them close.

The boy was really a young man of about fourteen years. He was delirious. His mother sat next to him on a stool holding a bowl so that when the boy coughed, he could expel his fluids into the container. As Wildrik approached, the child had a fit of convulsions and spat blood into the bowl before lying back to writhe on the bed. Wildrik drew back the coverings to look at the boy's skin and his worst fears were confirmed. There were tumours under his arms and further down around his groin.

The carpenter stood close by. "Can you do anything for him?" he asked. "It is though the devil himself has taken hold of my boy."

"The devil *has* taken hold of him."

It was not the first time Wolsenburg had suffered. Twenty years before, the plague had run rampant and had reduced the population by a quarter.

Wildrik helped those he could. He had no way of sparing their lives, but some of his patients lived, and he at least seemed able to make some of them more comfortable with his cups. He would use his knife to draw a small opening on the skin and use the cupping glasses to draw the excess humours away from the affected areas. He petitioned the city to make an infirmary close by in the country so that those taken by the disease could be isolated to keep the plague from spreading, and they agreed, allowing him to commandeer a manor nearby.

He fully expected that he would not live out the season, but prepared himself for the end with prayer, and he was reconciled to his sudden calling as physician. What was the clock to him in the face of such misfortune? Nearly everything, and he felt the loss that came from having his attention taken from it.

And then Albruna fell ill.

He came home and found her still in bed at midday. Her temperature was high and he did not need to examine her glands to know he would find the tell-tale nodules there.

He came to the bedside and kneeled, and he slid his hand under the coverings to find her fingers and to hold them.

She opened her eyes and saw him. "It's you," she said. "No other."

"I regret, My dearest, that I will not see your marvellous clock at work."

"I wonder if anyone will see it, but at the moment, it is the least of my concerns."

Albruna took a breath and struggled to raise herself to an elbow and Wildrik pulled a pillow to support her. "I would not like to consider that was true." She let herself recline and concentrated on him. "Think about your life, Wildrik. Do you really believe that it would have been good enough for you to toil in the fields or knot your muscles in labour without using that fantastic mind of yours? I said to you once that sometimes it is a good thing not to think too much, but often it is not a good thing to think too little either."

"Right now it is a good idea for you not to speak," Wildrik said. "You must save your strength."

Albruna fingered a bit of embroidery on the sheet. "I have been lying here aware that my heart will not beat for very many more days, and I have been thinking that I wish I knew what made it work. I am not afraid, merely curious, and that is something I take from you. I know that as you look at me now you see your wife and you also see a ready experiment. Surely you have something with you that you have not offered others. What is it? Something dangerous?"

"Ah. Yes. Were that I should know you a little as well as you know me."

"And?"

"Powdered emerald. Not dangerous but expensive," he smiled at her although the strain in his face told her nothing would truly lift his spirits.

"Wildrik, I can not say how much richer my life has been because I have spent it with you and your infernal curiosity. You have driven me mad with it, and I love you for that. For me, your clock is not a symbol of God's divinity, it is a testament to your ingenuity, to what can be accomplished through curiosity. I do not know what makes me live, but I am aware of what has made my life worth living."

The next day her fever was high and she was broken out in spots, purple at first, then blackening as the day wore on.

By the third day she was dead.

Unlike many of the victims who were carted away by sextons to be buried where space permitted, or burned outside the city, Albruna was to be interred in the cathedral cemetery, thanks to the influence of the bishop. The influence came from a distance, of course, because he had survived the plague by fleeing at the first sign of trouble.

When she died, Wildrik carried her to his workshop and stretched her body on his table there. He set by his apron of medical instruments and looked at her sallow, disfigured face.

Saliva welled up under his tongue and his mind began to race.

He picked up his blade and set to work.

By spring, the plague was over. The 1381 bout was less severe than the first torment years earlier.

Leon had survived, as had the carpenter and his wife and two of their children, one of whom, it turned out, was the young woman who had called Wildrik's clock a "toy". Her name was Fausta and she came to work for him as his housekeeper while he made the final preparations for the clock.

A marble cutter had made him an urn in the form of a phoenix which was to be installed to one side of the calendar dial. The urn was the reliquary and it was the last part of the clock to be added. It was laid in July when the rest of the orologium and the cathedral were almost finished. With great ceremony, on the night before the consecration of the cathedral, St. Peter's finger had been deposited there, along with three grains of incense and an attestation written on parchment, and the urn then sealed. Twelve candles were kept burning through the night while the Office of St. Peter was recited by the deacon.

Before the urn was delivered to the cathedral, Fausta and Leon helped Wildrik construct a false bottom in it, under which Wildrik placed a glass ball containing Albruna's heart.

It would rest there through the ages; as the clock marked time and signalled the motions of the universe, so Albruna's heart remained to keep its own regular beat.

In the dark of night, Fausta, Leon, and Wildrik listened to the chants of the deacon echoing to the arches of the structure, and then went home to sleep before the consecration of the cathedral in the morning.

Throughout the diocese, the day before the consecration was a day of fasting and abstinence.

"I don't mind the fasting much, but can't say I care for the abstinence," Leon said, snuggling up to Fausta, who slapped his creeping fingers. Theirs would be one of the first weddings to take place in the new cathedral.

At dawn, Matins were sung and candles lit under twelve crosses on the walls. The bishop anointed the crosses with holy chrism as he recited the form of consecration. He made three passes around the entire outside of the cathedral, sprinkling the building with holy water high on the walls, then low, and then even with his face. After each pass, he struck the doors and said, "Lift up your gates, ye princes, and be ye lifted up, ye everlasting doors, and the King of Glory shall come in."

On the first two passes the deacon inside asked: "Who is this King of Glory?" and the bishop answered: "The Lord, strong and mighty; the Lord mighty in battle" and then on the third said, "The Lord of Armies, He is the King of Glory."

The bishop then entered the cathedral and closed the door behind him and chanted a benediction while he traced the Greek and then the Latin alphabet on the floor.

The ceremony continued through the morning, the bishop growing weary with passes around the inside walls of the church, his voice strained with recitation and chanting. He consecrated the altar and then the clock, and the doors were opened to allow the people and the clergy in.

Wildrik, Leon, Fausta, and Fausta's family were led by an usher to a place of honour near the altar, among the nobility of the city and visiting dignitaries.

After the pillars were anointed, the twelve crosses were incensed, and the altar cloths, vases, and ornaments of the church were blessed.

The parishioners stood in the pews. "Is this going to go on much longer?" Leon whined. "My feet are killing me."

The ceremony continued with a high mass for St. Peter's Day, after which the bishop read an Indulgence of one year. Leon, whose Latin was rusty, asked Wildrik what it meant.

"It means you are forgiven," Wildrik said.

Leon looked disappointed.

"It also means you don't have to pay taxes for a year."

By the time the consecration ceremony was over, it was almost noon. Wildrik rose from his seat and proceeded to the clock. To start the works, he had to climb a ladder to an upper cabinet and engage the drive weights. As he ascended, the clergy chanted a psalm. He set the gears in motion just before twelve. He could sense the wheels stir and begin. The entire map of the works and systems of his clock unfolded like a galaxy in his mind. He knew every part of the clock, knew its relationships and interconnections. He knew when and how the figures would emerge from their hidden chambers, knew the formulae that would ring the carillon to play different hymns. He knew the plates of the sun and the moon and the stars, and he knew he held the secret of Albruna's heart inside himself, and that it was her memory, more than anything else, that kept his own heart beating.

He also knew that at the moment his heart was beating much more quickly than it usually did. He turned to face the congregation and hundreds of pairs of eyes turned toward him. They stared in wonder at the orologium, just as the works clicked and whirred, and the clock began to strike its first notes.

Entr'acte

Stimmler himself was nearly as fascinating a study as his clock. Partly, I believe, I have this impression because he was so entirely interested in me.

I decided some time ago, in a moment of honest self-realization, that I didn't much care for many of the people I was in regular contact with. It seemed to me then, that I could do without most of them. Here I refer largely to colleagues at work, acquaintances, and students. This is not to say that I disliked them, so much as I knew that it mattered very little whether or not they should maintain contact with me. I thought that, were it not for the practical situations that drew us together, I would probably not bother to speak to most of the people I knew, and certainly would not cross a busy street to greet them, even after an absence of years.

Perhaps this confession will make me sound like an uncaring soul, but there were people I was interested in, those I wanted to contact and, in fact, those I still do trouble myself to keep up with. The ones that interest me to that degree (this is the point I was going to make before my lengthy digression), the people I care to know, tend not so much to be interest*ing* as interest*ed*. I am not impressed by someone who, say, has spent a number of years travelling in India or working as a circus clown. I am more likely to have a meaningful conversation with someone who is full of wonder about what it would be like to spend years hiking the Andes, or training dolphins. What is life, after all, but a cascade of wanting to know?

Despite the frequent quiet in the cathedral and the hours I spent there in silent meditation while the only noise was the faint hum of motors and tires on the road outside and what I might describe as the life-breath of the clock — all its turning gears, clicking plates, and the whirr and chimes of its animations — there were other times when the place was packed full of, I suppose I should call them my fellows. For I too was merely a tourist come to gaze at one of the city's spectacles.

For some time, Stimmler continued to offer tours and answer questions. I heard him tell the same stories over and over, but each time with faint variations — not of the facts but of tone — so it seemed to me he was trying to keep himself interested in his work with these people. When I was present, however, he appeared to be telling his stories more quickly and answering questions with more abrupt answers, as though to hasten the hordes out the doors and get back to what he really wanted to do which was, I gathered, to spend time in discussion with me. I can say this with some authority because there were times when I had come unnoticed into the cathedral and had climbed the steps to the choir loft and had from there observed Stimmler giving these more leisurely tours.

I had extended my stay in Wolsenburg through the winter and then through the summer and, after war was declared, through the next winter as well. This I did for many reasons. The first of which was that I believed that my occupation of my friend's home was the only thing protecting it from being taken over, and that if I didn't stay, he would have nowhere to come back to once the trouble was over. Perhaps this act had not much to do with heroism, but it was genuine. It was difficult to measure the political winds in those days. A fruit vendor at the market who was an orthodox Jew simply failed to appear at his stall one Monday morning while an automobile repair shop proudly displayed the swastika above their bay doors and were clearly profiting from the German presence.

A further cause of my continuance was my work with the codex. I had been obliged to report to the Rathaus for an interview with Captain Möller of the Nazi administration and to surrender my foreign passport. Möller offered me tea in a china cup with blue cornflowers wreathing the saucer. He asked questions not so much about me as about my research — questions which I answered honestly. I was permitted to continue my study. Apparently, I represented little threat. I believed the codex to be authentic and wanted very much to be able to say so with absolute confidence. The book was a calendar which detailed agricultural schedules, but it seemed to me to be more than that. From what I could manage in the way of translation, it was also a sort of prophecy. The puzzle I was working to resolve was my own rather startling conclusion that the codex had in fact prophesied the current war, a conclusion which was most likely, but not certainly, due to my own immersion in the current events.

There was also Schpatz to feed.

Finally, I had become something of a henchman for Herr Stimmler. As the war progressed, Austria became more permissively part of the Third Reich. Jews in Wolsenburg were rounded up and I found myself increasingly part of a country that became stranger by the day. Only Stimmler and my apparent status as unthreatening shadow kept me from panic. When eventually Hitler launched his blitzkrieg and then France signed the armistice, it seemed as though the conflict might soon end. But the British humbled the Italians in North Africa and the Americans joined the war and the momentum began to shift. It became clear that the cathedral needed to be protected in case the city was bombed. Sacred as it may have been, the church was a distinct landmark; it was not likely to be a target, but we knew it would be used by pilots and bombardiers to locate other objectives. As a result of our fear of errant explosions, anyone able had been recruited to pile sandbags by the thousands along the walls of the cathedral as fortification, and Stimmler had made me his lieutenant in the safeguarding of the clock.

Although not a diminutive man, he had many of the qualities of an elf, including the slightly pointed ears that lifted from under his mop of greying hair, and especially the glimmer, or I should come right out and say "twinkle" in his eyes, because that is what it was.

He had a lovely way of sometimes answering questions directly and other times avoiding my eyes and merely hinting at a response as though to make me think he was giving me a chance to realize something I already knew, something that might later make me feel a fool for having had to ask, something that betrayed my limitless ignorance.

Such was the case when we discussed the devastating fire that raged through the city in the sixteenth century. It took three separate visits over the course of five days to extract the story from him and part of the difficulty appeared to come from his unwillingness to confront my ostensibly ridiculous question which was, "How does a stone cathedral burn down?"

Despite his reluctance though, I learned the further tale of the clock. It remains a mystery just how I learned it. However, I feel confident enough about the knowledge I acquired that I would trust myself to relate it if asked.

The mystery is this.

There is no small irony to me that much of the time I spent in the cathedral admiring the clock and studying and mapping its works passed in intervals I seemed unable to measure. On one instance, I might take what seemed to me to be a few moments to sketch one of the automata only to look at the time gone by and realize I had been engaged there for two full hours. Or, on other occasions, I might labour over a puzzle the gears in the basement presented me, tracing their pathways over and over as in a great court maze, until I could bear it no longer and would give up trying to understand the connections there. It would feel to me that I had been at that task for an entire morning and then would discover that, in fact, only a few minutes had passed.

Such gazing into intricacies may reinforce a sense of the meditative quality of my study of the great machine, so it may come as no surprise that I was often carried away in one reverie or another.

On one particular day, I had retired from a review of the ecclesiastical motor. I was resting in the pews, looking at the clock from the seats five columns back from the pulpit when there appeared, as if through the graces of a magician's smoke and mirrors, a young girl dressed in a brown frock and wearing a hood over her head so that it nearly covered her face. She was a rather strange-looking child — in that, though she was clearly a young girl of about ten years of age as the soprano lilt of her voice told me, the glimpses I caught of her face made me think she was considerably older. She spoke often like a ten year old, but at other times her manner of speech, the authority of her voice, and her certainty about the subject of her dialogue made me wonder just how old she was.

"Are you praying?" she asked.

"Not exactly," I said, "unless you consider meditating on this lovely clock a kind of prayer."

To my great surprise, she said that meditating on the clock was indeed a kind of prayer to her. In fact, she said, it is the only real kind of prayer there is. Without another word from me, she began, with no hesitation, to tell me the entire story of the rebuilding of the clock. Gradually, I began to realize that she was speaking as one who had been present during its construction in the sixteenth century.

Impossible, of course, and yet, she was so sure in her telling, so authentic, that I remained frozen in my seat, feeling like old Mr. Scrooge in Dickens' *A Christmas Carol* must feel when the ghosts of Christmas past, present, and future come to him as apparitions. She spoke and strolled past, without falter in her chronicle, and moved behind me so that when I turned to glance in her direction, she was but a silhouette before a stained-glass window, and because of the acoustics in the place, her voice seemed disembodied and to be coming from first one, then the other side of me. I was intensely curious about this little girl and was anxious to see her more clearly, perhaps to ask her to remove the hood.

She finished her tale just as the clock struck twelve and started into its most furious dance of the day. This distracted me and I glanced away from her only for what felt to me like a fraction of a second, but when I glanced back, she was gone.

The chiming clock told me that I had been sitting in the pew not very long at all, and yet the tale she told me took her the course of the morning.

When, a little later, I approached Stimmler and tried to find a way to tell him about my young visitor without having him immediately summon the authorities of reason, he cut me off and would not hear my account. He looked me squarely in the eye and said, "Now, I believe you had a question for me. What was it? Ah, yes, I remember. You wanted to know how it is that a stone cathedral can burn down?"

The Renaissance Clock — 1585

Grandma Theurl said I would be chosen, a star would shine over my birthplace and my arrival would be heralded by a chorus of angels. I suppose she was not altogether incorrect because Papa says when I was born, the midwife knocked over a candle and set the window drape on fire. All the noise and commotion set me to tears, and I cried non-stop for the first twelve hours of my life. Long after the fire had been doused, my wee voice disturbed him so much, he had to leave the house and sleep in the hen coop and he says he preferred the squawks and coos of the chickens to my relentless wails, even if he did go about all the next day with straw woven into his hair.

The first thing I remember about Grandma Theurl is being in her arms at night and looking up so her hair appeared to me as a net spread out against the sky, sea-blue in evening. The fish she was catching were stars.

She said the stars danced and she told me about their rhythms but she made me promise not to tell anyone else the things she told me. "Why not?" I asked her. "Why wouldn't you want everyone to know about the way everything spins?"

"I *do* want everyone to know," she said, "but the priests do not, so sew your lip closed, Angel."

That's what she called me sometimes, 'Angel.' My real name is Angeila, and I am called Geli, to keep it simple.

Grandma Theurl said I would have wisdom beyond my years. That may also be correct; it depends how I count years.

Just before my fourth birthday, when I was twenty-three years old, I wrote a diary note that went like this:

You would be wrong to think you do not have enough time,
there is always time and there is never enough
and that is why you look so sadly at the end of the day
because you feel that you are out of time
but you are not. You are not out of time and you
should not be unhappy. You are out of singing and dancing
and staying awake. You are out of bread and wine.
You are not out of candles. You should not be sad.
The sun will be back tomorrow. For now you can light the wick
and sing and dance without stopping.

My diary is full of Grandma Theurl's ideas. I had to put them somewhere. They were too big for my head and I was already having a hard time fitting all the dreams in there.

I wrote on a scrap of paper I pinched from the innkeeper, Ulrich, because I was just young and I thought, "What does he need all that paper for anyway?" and I suppose I still feel like that although I don't steal paper from him anymore.

I always tried to tear away the sheets without numbers on one side, but sometimes I could not help it and I realize now that weeks or even months of drinking debts may have disappeared without a trace.

Even Ulrich would not question me though. I suppose he feared there was more to lose than promissory notes by crossing me. What could I do about that?

I had proven myself to anyone who cared, even though I had not meant to. Once, hours before the sentries could see them, I warned the city of an army of insurgents storming towards the walls to demand sustenance. The city itself was a waif with a tight belt, so I let the word out and, to my surprise, they listened. Were it not for me, Ulrich would have lost all of his stores that day. So a scrap of paper here and there for me to practice my letters on was no great mischief to him.

The innkeeper had still greater ties to me. As a merchant, he depended upon his reputation as a fair and honest man, and a provider of homey comforts. His livelihood came from local patrons who appreciated the food and drink he provided, and his luxury came from the money he made stabling horses and laying beds for wealthy travellers. In the warmer months, the income from such guests could be considerable, but visitors were rare in winter and there were two other inns for them to choose from.

Before I met Ulrich, one of the other innkeepers devised a clever method of extracting the maximum fee from his most affluent guests: he tucked them into their beds which he had heated with warm stones, then gave them a libation laced with poisonous herbs so that they would be deep in sleep when he crept into their chambers later in the night and slit their helpless throats.

Over about ten years, this innkeeper laid to rest 185 such victims and stole every bit of the material wealth they carried with them. He had not been caught, but dozens of parties had arrived in Wolsenburg searching for their missing patrons and found their trail here grown cold, so that our city had begun to have a reputation as a haunted place among certain foreigners, particularly those from northern France, who, for no reason but luck and the fact that the innkeeper was fluent in their language, had amounted to the greatest number of victims in the slaughter.

That innkeeper had the unfortunate luck of meeting me in my second year when I was a budding young woman of fourteen. Upon making his acquaintance, I screamed and called him a murderer. I had seen him in a dream, not two nights previous, blood dripping from his hands.

When Grandma Theurl heard my prophecy, she demanded that the grounds around the innkeeper's property should be investigated, and it took not much digging at all before the bones of some of the many victims were uncovered in a most grisly excavation.

In the short term, of course, this discovery did little for the reputation of Wolsenburg as a welcoming locale, but, as the innkeeper was suitably punished by being publicly humiliated and having his insides turned out in the square, the assurance of wary travellers was soon re-established and Ulrich's business increased by over a third, the business from the executed innkeeper now shared between Ulrich and the well-behaved proprietor of the other nearby roadhouse.

As no one would any longer stay in the inn in which the bodies had been discovered, the building was taken over by the city and was renovated to become the district's first Leichenhaus in which the recently deceased, the recently *naturally* deceased, were laid out and watched for seven days before being laid in the grave as a way of guarding against the misfortune of premature burial.

Grandma Theurl said she needed a way to pass on her knowledge. She needed somewhere for her illustrations. I said she could just tell me because I could keep a secret. But she said that if I was already a precocious six year old when I had not yet even had my first real birthday, I would be an old lady like her in no time, and then what would we do?

"We will smoke tobacco in our pipes together, and laugh," I said. But of course she had a point. I became her apprentice anyway. She did not have much of a choice.

Grandma Theurl said she spilled some of the afternoone light on me when I was born and she was trying to put out the drapery fire. That's why I'm ageing seven times faster than other people. The afternoone light is one of the names for the elixir she was perfecting. "I guess it wasn't perfect yet when you spilled it on me," I said, "because it is supposed to make you live forever, not make you get old early."

Well, Grandma Theurl was not perfect, but she would be the first to tell you so herself.

She was not perfect, but she did not make many mistakes either. That is why I will never know if she meant for my flower to unfurl so quickly or not. She knew that the work she was doing could get her into trouble, even if everyone in Wolsenburg was afraid of her. It might be that she knew she was going to need help and I was the only one she trusted. Or it might be that she saw something in me and knew before I was even born that I would become her apprentice. That is one of the problems of being near someone who has second sight — you can never tell if they already know what is going to happen or not.

I usually find it best not to ask questions. My life went by seven times faster than other people's and that means I did not have the leisure to gain wisdom slowly or by a lot of trial and error. At ten years old, I was seventy and I knew that I would not be very much longer for the world than that. Already I was tired. Besides, Grandma Theurl was gone early and my work continuing her work was nearly done.

They said Grandma Theurl started the fire in the cathedral, but it was me. No one suspected because I was not yet one year old, but I arranged it nonetheless.

Before my first birthday, I could walk and talk and write and do some simple numbers.

It was Papa who taught me the numbers. His name was Villach and he was a professor of mathematics. That is why I learned so early. Grandma Theurl knew about numbers too; she is the one who instructed him, after all, but she would admit that he was better with them that she was. Papa could look at a wheel and, like a pigeon knows how many wingbeats will take it to the gable, know how many turns the wheel would have to take to get to the next village.

Grandma Theurl had learned her letters and numbers as a nun when her name was something different, but she left the nunnery to study privately with Nicholas Theurl. He was an alchemist who arrived at the nunnery and fetched Grandma Theurl away. He knocked on the door and when the mother superior asked him what he wanted, he pointed to Grandma Theurl and said, "I have come seeking the light that woman carries within her." So she collected her wool cloak and went with him without a word. She said she did not have to think about going and it did not seem to her that she was making a decision of any kind at the time. She went because she knew somehow that it was the right thing to do. "There are things," she said, "that you need not consider too deeply. At times, the mind can get in your way and you are better off simply being. We do not ask why we should breathe or drink and there are times in our lives when the rightness of the things we are asked to do is so self-evident to us, that we need not question them. Unfortunately, it is not always so, and the real trick of the Art is to know when to listen and to know when to stop and think."

They came to Wolsenburg and lived here in our little house on the furthest edge of the city where they were able to work at their experiments in peace in the laboratory at the back of the house. They had Papa and raised him without keeping their work a secret from him, but it was really only the numbers that he liked. "He is not one who is willing to dirty his hands or his soul," Grandma Theurl says, but I know she loved him anyway.

When Papa was a young man, Grandpa Theurl went away to Rome. He never came back. A messenger came with a paper that said he had died but before his body could be sent to Wolsenburg or buried in Italy, it disappeared from the casket. It was very strange. "Wondrous strange," Grandma Theurl said. The casket had been nailed shut and it took three men to open it. In Rome too, they are in the habit of a waiting period before burial. There, they check the corpse after three days to be certain it is truly dead. The vault Grandpa Theurl was in had also been sealed so his disappearance was a mystery and all Grandma Theurl did was smile.

Papa grew up and went away to study at the university in Paris, which should not, he says slyly, make him any better than anyone else, although I think it means exactly that. He met Mama there and brought her back with him. He loved Mama and says he always did. She didn't disappear when she died; she just burned up.

What Grandma Theurl taught me did not have much to do with the clock but the clock became my *lebenswerk*. It is a fortunate thing the cathedral itself did not burn down because I knew my life would not be long enough to have the whole building as my life's project. She loved the stars, their movements and shudders, and she never tired of saying that it was a travesty that the clock had been allowed to fall into disrepair.

At that time, it had been silent for half a century. She thought someone should make it work again. "When it was built, people thought it was a miracle," she said.

I argued with her. "But Grandma, you are the one who says people need to believe their eyes and not the illusions of the puffers."

"The puffers are one thing. False alchemists with their smoke tricks and sleight of hand deceptions; they beguile people deliberately to try to rob the innocent of what little savings they have." There is not much she disliked more than someone pretending knowledge. That might be the reason she had such a hard time with the priest. And that is why she surprised me like she did when she talked about miracles: "Miracles are something else. To rob people of their miracles is . . . well, it is simply cruel."

Perhaps it was then I realized I could not take Grandma Theurl for granted. I never pretended to know what she was thinking.

What I started to say about the funny way things work themselves out is that Papa was the one hired to restore the clock. It is because Papa knew mathematics that they wanted him. He had to figure out how to make Pope Gregory's new calendar fit into the restored clock.

Lucky for Grandma Theurl. I don't think the bishop would have been fond of having her at work in the cathedral every day. Given what happened to her, that is a certainty. But with Papa at work there, she could be moon to his tide and have an influence from a distance. She helped redesign part of the machine and as she helped Papa make the gears spin and whirr again, he helped her build her own kind of emerald tablet right there in the middle of the church.

Of course he had no idea she had anything to do with it.
As far as he was aware, I was the one helping him, and I was.
It is also true that Grandma Theurl was helping me help him.

Grandma had a little of the puffer in her that way.

Mother died while the fire was raging through the town.
It was not fire that killed her though. It was my little sister,
Esther.

Given all she knew about the miracles of life, it will always
be a mystery to me that Grandma Theurl did not care for
birth. She was in labour with Papa for two nights. "Two
nights of hell-fire and agony," she said. She survived, and
so did Papa, of course, but whatever happened over those
two nights tore something out of her so she was not able to
have any more children after Papa. I would never say so to
her, but I think perhaps that is why she would not attend
anyone else's birth, including mine. She was in her study
when she heard my first cries — that is how she came to have
the vessel with the afternoone light in it with her when she
burst into the room.

She said there are midwives who study long and hard
to help bring infants into the world and they are better
sponsors of birth than a woman with earth and ink on her
hands. It seems that the setting the curtains on fire at my
birth did little to change her opinion.

That is why she was with me at evening mass when Esther
was born. Grandma Theurl had taken me to prayers. We
went once a day, sometimes in morning and sometimes in
evening. It was a way to show others in the city that our family

was little threat to them because we knew that there were rumours everywhere. Grandma Theurl had used some of the Art to help other people. She would give mashed fenberries to someone with the retch and the next day they would feel better. Though they were always grateful and often came to her when they were desperate, they were also suspicious and she was wary enough to know that they could turn on her if she did not take steps to put them at ease. That proved to be true.

As I sat in the pew that evening, my mind wandered from the sermon. I had been thinking about how to help Grandma Theurl pass on what she knew. It had to be done in a way that was not obvious — with codes and symbols that could be understood by those who knew something about the Art, but symbols that others would read with innocence. A book was the obvious vehicle, but books were easily destroyed. Grandpa Theurl told us about an artifex who had been imprisoned for the last four years of his life and all of his books were nailed to the shelves in his laboratory and left there to rot.

The Maria Prophetissa laid down her wisdom in stone but that did not seem like a reasonable approach either.

I had a vision of a new clock, ornamented with new dials and figures that could be a moving map of all that Grandma Theurl knew. As she said, there are some things one need not consider deeply. All I had to do was crawl along the south gallery and move one of the candles there under a draped cloth. I could not have known it would burn so quickly or so well, or what chaos it would have created. Even Grandma Theurl had no idea it was me who started the fire, but when

Papa was given the commission for the clock, she began to wonder at the providence of it and made me confess. At first, she could not believe I would do such a thing, but then she nodded and looked at me again. "I will have to keep a different kind of eye on you," she said.

In the Great Work, one begins with the prima materia which is the unformed source of all things. As the fire raged through the cathedral, it was not hard for me to see that was what I had created there. Prima Materia. Chaos. Some people were screaming and running out the doors carrying children. Others were trying to put the fire out. In the midst of the fury, I overheard two men arguing about whether Holy water should be used to douse the flames.

It is unfortunate that there was not more Holy water around. A small brigade of men were engaged in carting burning pews out of the cathedral. These same men dashed the clock to the ground and tried to remove its burning spindles. I believe their efforts kept the roof from catching fire as the clock was the object that reached highest toward the ceiling and threatened to send sparks into the rafters. That is the real danger with a structure like the Wolsenburg cathedral; if the roof burns down, the walls may collapse inward and the whole of the building and hundreds of years of work will be lost. That was one of the things my not thinking first helped me ignore.

Removing the burning pews may have helped save the cathedral but it also spread the fire to the rest of the city. One by one, houses with thatched roofs burst into flame and then anything else that could burn did.

Mama was not at home. Instead, she had felt the pains
earlier in the day and had taken herself to the midwife's
because Grandma Theurl and I were already walking to the
cathedral and Papa was out visiting one of his fellow scholars.
When he returned, the neighbour told him where Mama
was. "Villach, you of all people should be able to figure out
what a pregnant wife, an empty house and no dinner adds up
to. She is gone herself to the midwife to have the baby. My
Anja went along and led her on our mule."

Papa ran out to find her and by then the fire had started.
The smoke was thick in the streets and people were running
everywhere. Usually, when there were big fires, everyone
who could move fled the city until the ashes settled and then
came back, used what they could of what was left and rebuilt
what was gone. It happened every few years so we all knew
what to do.

Papa arrived at the midwife's house just after Esther was
born. Mama was a silent boat of tears and the midwife
bustled about the room in a cloud of glowering humours.
The neighbour, Anja, held Mama's hand and rocked back
and forth. Little Esther was wrapped up in a sheet and she
was silent and still. She looked, Papa said, like porcelain.

Papa went to Mama's side and tried to clutch her, but the
midwife moved him. Anja stood and offered him Mama's
hand "like she was giving me a gift," he said, and she took
the opportunity to leave the room. The midwife was having
trouble stopping the bleeding and Mama was also beginning
to look like porcelain. She made Mama let go of Esther and

handed her to Papa. That's when he felt how still and lifeless she had come into the world.

The fire had spread. They could see out the windows that houses all around them were ablaze. Papa said Mama's eyes were empty but when she looked at him, she knew what he wanted. He put Esther down on the end of the bed and took gentle hold of the midwife who was desperately trying to press cloth against Mama to contain her blood. He pulled the woman away and asked her to go. At first she resisted but he said to her that two were already as dead and adding to the toll would not help the departed return.

He had her by the shoulders and gave her a gentle shove toward the door. She hesitated at the doorway and then turned and left.

Papa went back to the bed and picked up Esther and handed her to Mama and Mama gave him a little smile and sloped back against the tick, hugging Esther tight. He kissed her on the forehead and she closed her eyes and died.

The smoke was, by this time, creeping into the room like a tentative spirit so he made haste to be on his way.

It was several days before any of us went back to the city. Our house had remained unscathed but there was almost nothing left of the midwife's or of Esther or of Mama.

Tell the tale again and again and again
and again, in which One begets two, and two
becomes three, and three becomes the
fourth that represents the One.
One begets two, and two becomes three, and
three becomes the fourth that represents
the One. Again and again. Tell the tale
until the tail wraps around itself and, like
the lion who eats the serpent, is swallowed
whole.

That was one of the first things I wrote down when I began to study the Art with Grandma Theurl (on a page without numbers on the back, Ulrich would be glad to see). She welcomed my notes. She had her own books full of writing and illustrations where she wrote down descriptions and temperatures, trying to get things right.

It was after the cathedral fire that my apprenticeship with her began. I suppose she may have believed that if I was capable of burning down the clock in her service, I was able to help her with her craft.

She said it might have been better if our house, and in particular her laboratory, had burned down. "It would have been the third time the house has burnt and three is a good number, a provident number. Three becomes the fourth that represents the One."

By that time, nothing Grandma Theurl said surprised me anymore. People were rebuilding everywhere and since our house had not been damaged, and since Grandma Theurl was aging and I was still really a baby, we went about the city trying to help in whatever way we could — mixing poultices for burns, helping draw smoke from those who had taken too much of the fire in their lungs.

I know what I looked like, and though I did not once overhear a conversation about my appearance, I know people talked. How could I blame them? Before the first year had passed since my birth, I could walk and talk and write. I knew more already about numbers and making my letters than most of the adults would know in their lifetime.

Perhaps the worst was that I looked more like the elders in the city than the children. My skin was already becoming wrinkled, my hair was thin even then.

Now, I have very little hair at all and I look much, much older than I did, but even those years ago, looking in the glass made my heart sink. I *felt* like a child, but I was a caddisfly—young, vital larvae in an old, protective shell, awaiting transformation.

As soon as I knew I was not like the other children, which was quite evident to me after just three seasons, I began to adjust to the fact of my unusual life. And because Grandma Theurl made my early ageing seem to me like a great gift of wisdom, I did little to fight against it.

Before I began my study, Grandma Theurl made me memorize the code. She said these rules were not edicts but guides worth heeding. I divulge them only to show the honest nature of her processes and to expose the difference between a true artifex, a puffer, and a practitioner of dark arts.

An alchemist like Grandma Theurl is, first of all, chosen. As she was by Grandpa Theurl and as I was by her. Our only choice was to accept or refuse and it is no more a choice than accepting or refusing life itself.

The first tenet of the Art is discretion and silence, revealing to no one the nature of the operations. This code I break now against the wisdom of the ages and in Grandma Theurl's name.

Second, and as you see, well observed, is the isolation of the house in which the practice is undertaken, and third is the choice of days and hours when the labour might most easily be practised with caution.

Now come the rules. The fourth tenet is that of fortitude, diligence, and persistence. Without these qualities, the Great Work may never be achieved .

Fifth is the strict performance of standard practices and sixth is the use only of glass or glazed earthenware for heating, cooling and cleansing of the matter.

The seventh and eighth tenets are combined: that one must bear sufficient resources to pursue the Art and that one must not cohort with princes and nobles. These are the precepts that keep the Art true.

It is the puffers who consult with nobles. They take the Art which might one day offer much hope if the knowledge could be seen for what it is, a ladder to God, and they make it into a card trick. They are conjurors, no doubt, for they take the gold of greedy men and make it disappear with their promises.

The only noble we consulted with was Papa and he does not count. True, we came to require his resources, and his commission, but we did not deceive him with false promises, nor did we turn his gold into lead.

After Mama and Esther died, Papa lost much of his own will. He retired from his students because he could not face their questions. Part of his practice was to have the scholars he tutored correct his proofs and see if they could improve upon them. Where previously he had been gladdened to find a young mind that could find flaw in any degree of his thinking, it began to sadden him beyond reason. That his mathematics no longer seemed true to him was uncertainty he could not bear in the face of his growing doubts about his own existence.

He helped, as a labourer with the cathedral, rebuilding the pews and the altar. It was not much work, in fact, and was only months before services there resumed. Papa began to spend long days seated in the rows, staring uncertainly at the cross behind the altar. He would not kneel to pray and he would not take communion. He merely stared, mind a blank tablet.

It was early winter, midday when he was in his usual place, quite alone in the centre of the nave. He shivered from the cold, sat straight and said, "I need a new tunic and cloak."

It was that shiver that took him into the garment trade. Within a year, he had taken his savings and by careful bargaining and commerce, had turned them into a small fortune. He had two stations in the city where weavers produced fine wool cloth for him, and he had wagons leaving daily with the yield of his loom and returning from Venice and Genoa with silks and pepper, pearls and muslin. What he produced for a little, he sold for a lot, and what he traded in the cities to the south yielded him exotic goods so relished by the wealthy that he could name his price for them.

In these labours he excelled, but in them he was also swallowed.

Grandma Theurl's laboratory had a stove at one end. We were proud of it because it backed onto the wall with the enclosed stove in the kitchen of the house. It was not something to be flaunted, but a stove, rather than a hearth, was a luxury Grandma Theurl made me sure to appreciate, and she let me know that few of the other houses in the city were as fortunate as ours in this regard.

My studies in the Art continued even while we worked on the clock, our industry was merely richer for it, and our days and nights longer. I never tired of working with Grandma Theurl and of listening to her stories.

By my middle age however, and by that I mean in my fifth year when I was as thirty-five or forty is to most, it became clear to me that I must adapt her methods for myself. Her way of the Art was the way of the snail up the tree and I simply did not have time to follow her ruminative practice.

Papa's work in textiles brought him together with other merchants who he may not otherwise had any reason to have dealings with and people who, I feel, led him to lose his brightest feathers to the foxes. I may as well name the worst culprits then, had I not?

It is Herr Frugger I blame most. I do not pretend that Papa was wholly innocent, nor that he aspired to the same gifts as Grandma Theurl. As I have said, it is true that the pursuit of the Art chooses us more than we choose it, but I believe that Papa is, at heart, good.

From his first excursion to Venice, the others could see that his gift with numbers could be its own kind of treasure to them. Not only did he know that a fortune is made by shaving one coin at a time from the price at which one purchases goods and by adding one coin at a time to the selling price, but he was also of a practical mind where others let their dreams or their greed lead them asunder. At Venice, he saw Northern goods prepared for export destroyed before they could be shipped. Tables and cassone made of wood from our forests were splitting in the heat and moisture on the pier, astrolabes and ironworks rusted before they could be delivered. He determined to keep Northern goods for Northern trade and to barter his own wares before the risk of sea transport was an issue. He let other merchants risk their fortunes taking goods afar. He would go no further than Venice himself and is proud that he has never set foot aboard a ship.

It is with that principle that he built his riches and, as a just and fair man, he willingly shared his wisdom with other merchants in Wolsenburg. That is what lifted him highest in eyes of the traders, and that is what also was his undoing.

He described for me his first visit to Venice and his residence there at the Fondaco de' Tedeschi. He said from his perch on the third floor of that rich building on the Grand Canal, he could see the ships setting sail and coming in to port. Stores were piled everywhere, nothing came in small bundles; there was only excess. Wine and cheese and fish and paper to be shipped to the East were stacked on the docks, not just hundreds of barrels of wine but barrels by the thousands, and even by the tens of thousands. Rounds of cheese big as cart wheels were stacked in legions, and entire ships laid low in the water with a ballast of nothing but herring bound for Turkey.

Venice itself sounded like a marvel to me. Imagine, a whole city afloat on the sea! He said the cathedral San Marco is more splendid even than our own cathedral and not only that, but it is but one of many in the city.

I regret that I will never see Venice, but my travels have been wide without the need of leaving.

If Papa did well trading his cloths there, he did not go without misfortune. His association with Herr Frugger was our salvation, it is true. It is Herr Frugger who made Grandma Theurl's work on the clock possible, but it is also Herr Frugger who steered Papa away from us forever. Papa gained his fortune in Venice, but he lost his soul, and the work I have yet to do, is to forgive him.

After the fire, Grandma Theurl and I retreated to our studies the way a wolf will withdraw from its kill after it has fed. Though I have already said that my intention behind the fire was clear to me from the moment of insight, we also knew that we could do little to hasten the reconstruction of the clock. No one in the civic orders would have heeded our advice and we wanted to draw no attention to ourselves. My trust in the providence of events is no different than yours or any other good Christian's. It is faith.

I do not know what stilled the clock. It had marched on, keeping time despite time, for a century and a half before something in its machinery stopped working. Clockmakers were brought in, and astronomers, and mathematicians, not long after the clock failed, but they were puffers in their own right and were content to drain off whatever resources they could from the city before they admitted defeat and left with their tails low and their purses full.

It is these failures that kept the clock idle for two generations, but after the fire, a new spark was lit in many important eyes at once.

What can I divulge about alchemy that will help my faith make sense?

The first thing is that time is of the essence. Had the clock been working, it would have helped Grandma Theurl predict the best time for beginning the remaking of the clock. The time must be coordinated with the stars or the work is doomed to failure from the start. The best time for the beginning of most things is when Aries or Taurus are rising — spring, when renewal and fresh beginnings suggest themselves everywhere.

I was not unaware of this circumstance when I lit the cathedral drape on fire, however, neither had I done anything to consult with the astral bodies before I acted. And yet, Grandma Theurl later told me that I could not have chosen a better time.

It begins with an end. The first stage of the work is called Nigredo — the blackening. There is a first material which, for our work with the clock, was simple enough to acquire — it was the clock itself, or at least some of the charred remains of it.

When Grandma Theurl and I returned to the city after the fire, we stopped at the cathedral before we even went home. We merely needed parts. It was best if we could no longer tell what they were, as long as we were sure they were from the clock. Grandma Theurl plundered handfuls of ash and bits of gears into a sack and we were about to leave when I dusted off a marble urn that was in the shape of a phoenix.

Of course, the phoenix is the bird that rises reborn from the ashes. It was another instance of acting without hesitation and without thinking. "Take it," Grandma Theurl said. It was only later that we learned the urn was the reliquary for the cathedral and that we had stolen St. Peter's remains.

I am truly sorry for the scandal that caused, but we had every intention of returning the remains to the clock all along.

The blackening begins with an end or a death. There was the end of the clock and in this case there was also the death of Mama and Esther. First, there is the cleansing. The heating happens in the egg — a glass flask which contains a liquid we have distilled over years. To this, the prima materia, the clock dust, is added. This is heated and cooled by degrees, and its progress is measured. During this part of the Art, Grandma Theurl and I made many preparations with ourselves so that when the time came, we would be ready.

Our work was a partnership. The ideal assistant for Grandma Theurl would have been a young boy, not me, because part of the Art is a balance of the male and female. Perhaps for Grandma Theurl, working with a woman who was also a baby was already complicated enough.

The blackening continues for quite some time. In this case, it was two and a half years. Two and a half of your years, not mine. I should be clear. By then I was twenty-one — or three years old if we want to continue to count your way — and I had learned much about the Art. Only then did we finally produce what we wanted to, a glow from within the centre of the matter. It was me who did it, in fact, and at first I felt a little badly for Grandma Theurl who had worked so hard all that time, but Grandma Theurl was pleased. By then, what interested both of us even more was the glow in Herr Frugger's eyes.

Again, I was merely lucky when I burned the clock. Not only was the season right for renewal, but the century as well. What I did not know when I lit the fire, was that Pope Gregory had just that month issued a papal bull to change the calendar. October fourth of that year was, according to his decree, to be followed immediately by October fifteenth.

The point was to make the calendar work right and at least that change got it a little closer.

Well, all of Europe was rattling the cage of time about the change. Working people were afraid they would lose ten days' wages if they followed the new calendar — many could not be convinced that they would not have to work those days because those days would not, in effect, be days. And landlords everywhere prepared to collect for the extra ten days despite the fact that they did not deserve rent for a period of time that was not.

The prince of Wolsenburg, after talking to his civic advisors (or, in other words, the merchants who allowed him to stay in power), and in concert with the bishop, agreed that Wolsenburg would join the new system if only to simplify trade with other countries.

The change itself went fairly smoothly in Wolsenburg. In other cities, there were riots and large protests, but here it was October and a chill was in the air. Certainly, the new calendar was one of the only topics of discussion in the markets, but most accepted it without a fight.

Still, the space in the church where the clock used to be and the remains of it still standing that were left as a reminder rested like a yawn in the city's memory until Grandma Theurl and I finished the first part of our work and Herr Frugger began to shine at the fall carnival.

The carnival was something everyone looked forward to all year long. Twenty nations were represented there. Imagine that. Whole streets were given to booths for one trade or another. By this time, Papa had factors working for him and could dedicate himself to overseeing his trade business from a distance. He could also do at the fair what many of the others could not do — enjoy himself. The street where his wool factor had the booth was lined with other wool merchants, over a dozen of them all told. One had come all the way from Scotland and was a spectacle for all to behold because his hair was red as a poppy. I could not help but laugh even though I was the last person who should be laughing at the appearance of others.

There were leather merchants, wine merchants. People selling all varieties of cloth and fabrics. The best were the silks! The finest flow as water does and are light as lark's breath although they hold in heat when wrapped about the skin. If there are witches among us, I say let the silk merchants be burned, for how else could they make such impossible raiments?

Along other streets were row upon row of spice merchants so that gusts of their wares threatened to overwhelm and incite passersby to dreams of exotic lands where two suns rise in the east and dragons lash out from the very edges of the world.

I know of not one soul who could resist the gaiety of these days. Grandma Theurl made no attempt to reproach the affair and instead joined in head-on by occasionally drawing forth three coloured glass balls from her poke and juggling them before what gathering she might wish to entertain. She took special pleasure in finding ways to upset the astronomers, conjurors and other puffers who set up stands to use their ridiculous card tricks to try to convince the unwary that if they could change a queen into a king, then they could also change a silver coin into gold.

The windy Franciscans she let be, although she also disliked their "idle thundering to the crowds" as she called it. And the singers and players she celebrated, using her most subtle persuasions to encourage those bent on spending their money to give it to the musicians before one of the variety of public or private thieves could steal it away.

Not far from the cathedral, the money-lenders established themselves at their tables with their cash boxes and ledgers. It is a good thing I did not borrow any of their paper for my journal. Who knows what fortunes might have changed had I done that.

Naturally, when the merchants had finished their business for the day, they either joined in the revelry or retreated to the ale houses where they held forth about the strengths and weaknesses of this or that leader, the problem with x or the solution to y, and the always popular topic, what was to be done about the impetuous guilds that were making it so difficult for an ordinary merchant to keep his vaults stocked with riches?

That was where Papa found himself at the end of the day, seated next to Herr Frugger who had been so seated most of the day and had already consumed thrice his usual daily portion of wine and ale. Though the glow in him was born of easy spirits, I recognized it nonetheless. That is when I saw my opportunity and found a way to have him raise the issue of remaking the clock.

I sadly confess that Papa had learned all the bad habits of excess that go along with being a merchant. He had grown portly with overeating and drinking, and was not unfamiliar with the after-effect in the morning of too much revelry.

I had come looking for him in the ale house after leaving Grandma Theurl to make her way home. Disgusted with the carnival and having done enough damage to the soothsayers for the day, she was content to go back to her work, but I felt compelled to stay out and was not one to fight such compunctions in myself.

Rather than approach the table directly, I sat far enough away from the men that they did not notice me and close enough that I might listen in to their conversation.

Herr Frugger was speaking with such animation about the pope's calendar that he flopped his arms across the table like loose eels, nearly spilling all of the tankards and cruses arranged there.

As the serving-woman was pouring ale at another table nearby, she was looking at Herr Frugger with unkind eyes. He had undoubtedly offended her with his hands in some way, perhaps very recently. She leaned over to serve and I whispered, just loud enough for her to hear, that if Herr Fruger had a clock of his own, he might be able to read not only the pope's new time, but also be able to judge when he should be better off at home with his wife than fondling servants in the ale house.

She turned to Herr Frugger and repeated what I had said, and offered it to him as a challenge.

The other men at the table, including, I am sorry to say, Papa, cooed marvellously at her impertinence. Papa laughed so hard, he even spit out a draft of ale which just missed Herr Frugger. The woman stood her ground and before Herr Frugger had much of a chance at all to react, another of his party spoke up rather seriously and said, "The woman is bold, but true. It is a shame that even our old cathedral clock, which was once a symbol of glory for Wolsenburg, is now but a scrap heap and an embarrassment."

The laughter was suddenly abated and there was a new clucking and cooing around the table. Herr Frugger had become the wealthiest man in Wolsenburg, and indeed in the province, because he was adept at reading, among other things, the tides of public desire. Before long, he was talking as if the idea of restoring the clock to its former glory had been his all along.

"Who would be capable of performing such a task?" he said, wagging his jowls as he spoke. "Surely we shall have to look far and wide for someone who is sufficiently skilled."

And that is when Papa sat up and shook off the mist of drink that had settled like autumn fog across the lowlands of his mind and said they would have to look no further than the table at which they sat. "If you, Herr Frugger, can provide the necessary funds, I will build you a new clock."

Unfortunately for Papa, the next morning dawned brightly. He had come home rather late and the dawning sun blinded his swollen eyes.

And unfortunately for me, I could see that his mind was a swept room — he had no memory at all of his promise to fix the clock or of anything else from the previous evening, and so I had, with no tact at all, to remind him. When he had managed to steady himself enough to rise and dress and come to the table, I rather unnaturally threw my arms about his neck and said, "Papa, I am so proud of you for accepting Herr Frugger's commission to build the new cathedral clock."

He looked puzzled at first but I saw the light grow in him but as it did, I saw all of the objections that the wine and ale had hidden, boil frantically to the surface. "I am afraid that was a rather exuberant promise, made in haste and without reason," he said. "I shall have to tell Herr Frugger that I was mistaken. I have trade to attend to and no time to trifle with machines such as that."

"Then let me do it," I said.

"Let you do it?" he snickered and looked at me, and snorted and chuckled and went so far as to guffaw. Then, seeing the expression on my face, he looked at me again.

"Really, Geli. You can not possibly be serious. Do you have any idea of the work that will be involved?"

"Yes," I said, and deposited my drawing of the astrolabe dial on the table in front of him.

"But Liebchen," he said, shaking his head.

"Look at the drawing, Papa. I have others as well. In fact, I have an entire design completed."

He paused as he looked at my drawing. I could see that he was checking my figures. He paused some more and then proceeded to say absolutely nothing. He was absorbed in my sketch.

"Papa?"

He appeared to wake from a dream and he shook his head. "It is good work. It is fabulous, good work. But that does not erase the fact that you are a mere three years old. Just how do you think I will convince Herr Frugger that a child should be given the funds for a project that will take several years to complete and involve several dozen artisans?"

I told him is was really very simple. There was no need to tell Herr Frugger or anyone else anything. I would do the work and would keep him informed. He would make contact with anyone else who needed to be involved, and I would do all the rest. That way he could keep at his trade and, I added — mischievously I admit — we might even make a little profit.

The Art has two divisions and four main stages. The first division is the lesser, and the second is the greater.

Within the lesser Art are the two stages of nigredo and albedo which some refer to as the blackening and the whitening. After the blackening, the initiation of the matter, comes the whitening, or cleansing. Then, in the division of the greater Art, there are two more stages, citrinitas and rubedo; the yellowing and the reddening. These stages involve a second initiation of the matter, this time in its cleansed form, and then the final union of elements which combine to produce the new matter.

I cannot say in terms clearer than this what it is that Grandma Theurl and I were doing in the lab with our heated vessels. Any other fellow of the Art would need to find a different way to the same end. One's own way, for that is all there is—a path that no one else might follow.

And from our work, flowed the design for the new clock. It is not wise to record the practice of the Art literally. Any other alchemist must find her own way to the same end so it is simply not possible to provide the recipe books that the rich and powerful request. Many of our number have been carried away by force and locked in towers because nobles thought they had captured someone who would do service turning lead into gold.

Others have been captured as witches, and that is a more grisly end as I have seen.

No one, except perhaps me, could understand Grandma Theurl's notebooks. But because what we do is of necessity a practice of solitude and silence, it is useful for another true artifex to have at least some guides to help them trust the knowledge they gain working at the Art.

That is why the clock was such a perfect conveyance for Grandma Theurl's knowledge. It sits in a public place and anyone can see it there. No one who spent hours and hours studying the symbols embedded in the clock would be seen as suspicious. No, they would be seen as pious instead! How could it be any better?

That is how the new clock came to be so intricately, and some said curiously, adorned.

For me, the mathematics necessary for calculating the measurements and movements came suddenly and quickly. I decided it would not serve me well to tell Papa that the drawings and the very finest details about the gearing and pin-motions had been completed, by no one but me, in a little over a week. I do not even know how I managed; by not thinking I suppose. I even calibrated the leap years according to Pope Gregory's new calendar and there was not a clock in all of Europe that had yet been fixed to do that.

Even for him, it would have been perhaps two years' work. When he took my drawings to the best clockmakers in the province, they confirmed the quality of my innovations and told Papa that he was indeed a very brilliant man. It gave me no end of pride to see him bathing in that glory.

From the beginning to the end, work on the clock went well. It took three years to complete which may seem swift to you but was, you will remember, twenty-one years of my life.

When it was finished, it was radiant and as impressive to the bishop as it was to Grandma Theurl. Herr Frugger had stayed true to his promise and provided all the funds the clock required, so there was much gilt and pearl. The sun and the moon, the tree, the dragon: these were represented in clever ways in the dials and also in the moving figures that provided the clock's entertainment and song. We had even managed a representation of the Maria Prophetissa herself along with illustrations of her tablet text. To others, she looked like the Holy Mother so all were pleased.

To point to the correct day on the date dial, we had an oak Mercury made holding a silver spear. The arm could be lifted and lowered to indicate the moveable feasts. The placement of this figure was most important to us because Mercury represents the Art itself.

At twelve on the clock each day, a golden egg opened to reveal an old king who himself was split apart to reveal a young and vital prince emerging from within.

Some of the other adornments were, for Grandma Theurl and I, the very purpose of the clock, not an addition to it.

Oh, of course we made all the dials and gears to chart the progress of the moon and the tides and the stars, but I hoped the clock, rather than proclaim when people should come or go or plant or harvest or eat or sleep might instead encourage them to look elsewhere for such direction.

Here my story should end in splendour. The clock was completed, consecrated, celebrated. Once again, people came from great distances to marvel at it. Alas, there is a sadder end.

Grandma Theurl's Greater Work proceeded all the while the clock was being constructed, as did my apprenticeship and my own Art.

It was true though that I could not be as engaged as I would have liked. Although Papa was wise in numbers and could genuinely and easily understand my schematics, and could explain them to the artisans who had to forge the gears and parts, my presence was still often required. And, as we wanted no one to know that the designs were mine (or Grandma Theurl's through me), we often had to consult in private in great detail so he could be certain enough about the work to answer anyone's questions.

That Papa and I were so often in the cathedral showed our innocence to the Inquisitors when they came, but the same was not true for Grandma Theurl.

After the fire, the leaders in the church were as distracted as a colony of bats in a rainstorm about what needed to be done. Unlikely as it may seem, no one thought about the missing reliquary. It was the phoenix we had taken from the clock's remains. That too was an action without thinking. We took it because it was a phoenix; one of our symbols of transmutation and of the Great Work itself.

I can not explain fully what happened to it in the following years except to say that by pure carelessness, the phoenix was neglected and fell by the wayside, under a table in Grandma Theurl's study.

Until one of the choristers noticed it was not part of the new Wolsenburg cathedral Clock. As a child, he had been fascinated with the phoenix and, admiring the new clock one day as he climbed the stairs, he said in passing that he wished the new clock had maintained that small feature which had always been his favourite.

The priest overheard him and was immediately struck by the realization that not one soul had even asked about the church's relics since before the fire. It was he who summoned the Inquisitors.

I cannot say what thoughts led Papa to his accusations, for I did not speak to him, neither at Grandma Theurl's trial, nor at her execution.

The truth was simple enough, she had the reliquary in her laboratory and he had seen it there. Why not then take the path of courage and simply return it quietly to the church in the dead of night? Why lead the Inquisitors to our door, as he did, when he knew well that her practice in the Art would be seen as witchcraft?

What they did to urge her toward confession is a story that would pain any ear like a pin in the drum, and will pain too the teller of the tale.

She was arrested. The laboratory and all of her work and mine too, was destroyed. They tore her clothing from her because they believed that foul spirits could hide there, and paraded her through the streets. At once, a fury was unleashed. Dozens of men and women, all whom had been offered cures and remedies and who had accepted them gladly in their own dark hours, appeared on the path to taunt her and profess her guilt. They offered her a cleansing of her soul by forcing open her mouth, inserting a wide funnel, and then dropping upon her tongue and the back of her throat, a burning coal from the fire. After that cruelty, what innocence could she declare?

They used the strappado which you may know as simple and extremely effective. Her hands were bound tightly behind her back, and then the rope was tossed over a beam. This they lifted slowly until the arms dislocated within the shoulder sockets and she was lowered down again.

I do not know what they wanted to hear from her. I am told there are documents of this trial that make it sound as though a confession of her commerce with the devil would have excused her from further punishment, but I think they wanted to make her pay for the insult to their saint.

With the rippers, they tore her breasts from her chest, while at the same time they used the pear to shred her woman's nest, turning it like a key until its sharp wings unfolded inside her. All of this she withstood, so it was some relief to me when at last they burned her.

From her ashes rose my Art.

My wish was to leave the city, but my instincts made me stay. Here I had been treated as innocent, a stroke of fortune I guarded carefully. I used the remains of her laboratory to quietly build my own. While Wolsenburg slept, I weaseled in and out of doorways back to the cooling remains of the pyre and collected the ash of her body for my crucible. I watched the flame heat liquid and mixed the components. I worked toward my end. I spoke to no one again.

What good is it to speak of her innocence now? It is that within the womb of the earth is where gold grows, and that true measures are measures not of clocks but of plants, and seas, and stars, and shifting stones; that within nature is all creation and my work has been to help her — nature, mother of us all — to perfect herself by beginning with me and my own prima materia and looking there within for the golden spark of the divine.

Second Intermission

It was truly a gift of circumstance that I came to be in Wolsenburg for the change from winter to spring. My first April in the city was grey and occasionally wet, and yet the freshness of the new season was upon even the dampest days. Rain was punctuated by a kind of opening so that to walk about during or just after a brief storm was to be assailed in the most pleasant way by the scents of flora coming into its own. If the only blossom in the city were the lilac, it would have seemed too much to me, but over the centuries the gardens here have been cultivated to nurture the most sensual orchestra of fragrance so that one must stop often on a walk by the canal simply to try to sort out the variety in any given breeze. It is the olfactory equivalent of walking into a tropical aviary in the zoo and trying to hear all the species' songs of the birds at once.

Perhaps my time in Wolsenburg had released me from a state of being in which I might once have attempted to escape such stimulation, and perhaps it was the clock itself — an overwhelming experience if there ever was one — that opened a previously closed part of myself to any and all experience. I drank in everything as if emerging from a complete desert of a life. My desire to taste, smell, touch, hear, and see everything, everything, everything, was unquenchable. I had never felt so very much alive, and — this is a confession — I had never before wanted to be alive so much, despite the military conflict raging through Europe. Perhaps it was the propinquity of death that sent me reeling towards life more fervently than ever before.

I have had my share of dark periods, and I believe the darkest among them were from doubt. In my younger days, my student years particularly, I was Goethe's Faust, tossing out for reason's sake any and all faith in the divine, and replacing it with an unwavering belief in science and empiricism. I see now that my need for proof was reckless fanaticism.

Still, it is research and my desire to understand that led me to marvel at the wonders of the world. The more I came to understand sculpture, chemistry, music, biology, literature, and physics, the more surprises I found there. It is science and art that led me increasingly to marvel at human ingenuity, and yet it is love that allows me to trust in the intricate pattern of circumstances that makes that ingenuity possible.

So it was with wonder that I stumbled for the first time upon the Botanischer Garten at the edge of the old city a full eight months after my arrival in Wolsenburg and five months before the beginning of the war. It is a remarkable place where time unfolds by the moment in the greening of leaves; by the day in the opening and closing of blossoms with the light; and by the season in the bursting forth of bulbs from underground. I continued to visit there as often as I could. It was no small irony that I found sanctuary in the garden when I had had too much of Stimmler's stories or explanations of the clock — he had taken it upon himself to educate me about the most minute workings of it — so that I sometimes needed to flee the cathedral. Every time I felt that I had come to be familiar with the garden, I came across some new species of plant or flower previously unknown to me. Even in the winter, the Botanischer Garten was a lovely place to stroll and when, after three years in Wolsenburg the Nazis took the codex away from me, the garden is where I went to mourn the loss of my project. I found myself weighing the pure folly of having stayed so long, spending evenings with Schpatz on my lap, and days holding up walls and helping adjust the delicate gears that agitated in their cases while bombs dropped all around from planes flown by my own countrymen. By this time I had become something of an apprentice to Josias Stimmler. As I became more and more interested in the clock, Stimmler allowed me greater access to it, and my impulse had been to work toward the goal of understanding it completely.

Perhaps it was providence that put an end to my work with the codex; if so, it came in the form of Captain Möller. He had obliged me to report to him monthly about my progress with my research. At each meeting he offered me tea in the delicate cornflower cups and he poured the milk and added lumps of sugar for me. I had calculated that my best strategy was to appear as neutral as possible, hoping that my attention to antiquity would spare me from the suspicion of espionage.

Before our last meeting, a messenger arrived at my door to request that I bring all of my notes, observations, calculations, and letters with me to Herr Möller's office. This I did, assuming that Möller's interest was growing along with my own excitement as I became more confident in the authenticity of the codex. I reported to his office with my materials in a cardboard box, prepared for an extended lecture in pre-Columbian astronomy. I was naive. Möller poured the tea as usual, but rather than lean forward on his seat like a student anxious for wisdom, he reclined in his armchair and crossed his legs in a gesture of insouciance while he stirred his tea and said, "You will leave these materials with me. A scholar at the University of Leipzig has taken an interest in your work and wishes to verify the codex for himself. I'm sure you understand." I tapped my teacup into the saucer with such shocked conviction that the handle of the cup broke off like a piece of icicle coming away from an eave. Speech was beyond me and it is just as well that it was. "It is terribly unfair," he said to me, "however, I am following orders of my own and you would do well to heed them without spilling any . . . more tea." That was all. Except that the Leipzig scholar discounted my work and declared the Egger codex a hoax. The manuscript was then destroyed when Leipzig was bombed and any hope of completing my project was ruined forever.

In truth, when the codex was removed from my study, I had already turned most of my attention to the clock so it provided me with very little reason to leave and more than one good argument in favour of remaining. And then I found another.

Her name is Leesa Haspel. We met at the puppet house.

In the middle of Wolsenburg's Botanischer Garten there is a marionette theatre that has been in use since the middle of the nineteenth century, run by generations of Haspels. Leesa bears the tradition these days and is a master (if there is a female equivalent for this word, I do not know it) puppeteer.

I happened upon the theatre on my first walk through the gardens and arrived just as a play was about to begin. I paid my entrance and was escorted to a seat at the rear of the theatre. Only children are permitted in the first ten rows and adults, particularly those on their own, must sit at the back so as not to impede any small person's view. My knees were buckled nearly to my chin on the small bench and I was like a giant in a pedal-car. It was a Saturday afternoon and the rows ahead were packed with children. The seating arrangements took some little while and as the scheduled time for the performance came and passed, the children began to chant, *"Auf mit dem Erscheinen; auf mit dem Erscheinen."* It was splendid.

The lights went down and the children cheered. As soon as the curtains opened, they became completely silent. The magistrate of the town "walked" onto the stage and *Puss in Boots* began. I do not know whether I was more enraptured by the sheer glee of the children as they laughed and cheered, answered the cat's questions and taunted the prince, or by the wonder of the performance itself.

Leesa, I have said, is truly an accomplished puppeteer, and the movements of her players are so graceful — I was going to say lifelike, but that is not quite right. They have a life of their own, and part of what makes them wonderful is the sense of *not knowing* how it is that one person could operate so many puppet-actors at one time and provide them with all the character achieved in their unique and subtle gestures.

So it was that, hunched over on that little seat as the play progressed, two extraordinary things happened to me: I fell in love with a woman I had not yet seen, and I unclosed myself to the divine.

Though I say these things happened to me in the puppet theatre, I might also say that it is the Wolsenburg Clock that was most responsible for these revelations. I wanted to know what every gear was for. I wanted to trace backward to make sense of all of the maker's calculations. I wanted my intellect to be able to match that of the man who had made the thing in the first place.

It is a paradox that real knowledge is somewhere beyond the mind. In order to fully understand the clock, I needed first to let go of the notion that there was only one way, the scientific method, to understand the great machine. The more time I spent with the clock, the more I came to be acquainted with it as a living thing and the more I came feel that wanting to know is all there is; that sometimes the mere wanting is more reasonable than tying up thought in a comfortable, illusory knot.

It is an analogy I have used with students to discuss approaches to art in classrooms. To look closely at the way a drawing, painting, or illumination is constructed is not to "take it apart," as they are so fond of saying. It is to examine those parts to see them more deeply. And yet that process can not replace the initial viewing of a piece — the "ah ha" revelation of a juxtaposition of images that is surprising and just right, when an observer is led toward understanding him or herself in a brand new way without having asked. If I were to take apart the Wolsenburg Clock, I could never get it to function properly again. What I want is the same thing I want from Cezanne's paintings: to look closely into the works with even greater wonder, and never to make it stop.

In allowing myself to relax the strictures of understanding I had placed on my mind and instead to allow myself primarily to marvel at the clock, I had another epiphany: the clock is God.

Here, I had been looking at the device as a remarkable machine, cleverly constructed to reproduce complicated movements in the universe. Some of these movements are so intricate, in fact, that one mechanism that drives the celestial globe (which mimics the movements of the stars around the earth) is designed to account for the gyration of earth's axis in a 25806 year cycle!

And yet the architect of the current clock, Jean-Auguste Stimmler, forefather of the present keeper, never intended (I am certain of this) the clock to be a display of his ego. He did not want someone like me to come along nearly two hundred years later and revere *him*, he wanted me to allow into my life *Him, Her, Them, It*, or *Whatever* it is that we might in a more secular way accept as the Divine.

To the left of the clock is the altar and the statue of Christ on the cross. I mean no offense to Christians, but in all the time I have spent in the cathedral, I have born witness to the faithful praying intensely and in each case, there is something vital in their meditations. However, the vitality has seemed to me very clearly invested in the parishioners; perhaps the prayers are directed outside them, but that — what shall I call it? — life energy, emerges most definitely from *within* and is projected out toward what I can only see as the lifeless, carved stone that is a representation of Christ.

And there to the right of the altar, seeming much more like an addition to the main event, is the clock, its chest puffed up, its own arms open, and its labyrinth of mechanisms constantly in motion. Emerging from within the clock is a vitality not unlike the prayers of the faithful, so that the more time one spends with the great machine, the more deeply one is led to wonder at it. Once every four hundred years, it accounts for the Gregorian leap-year rule with one turn of a distinct gear. A gear in the ecclesiastical register (which calculates the moveable feasts) turns once every 2500 years. The animations must be seen to be believed. My favourite, naturally, are the Monks who scribe the book of Genesis as if writing the story for the first time.

This sense of wonder, you see, was Stimmler's purpose. All the while I had been marvelling at his invention, I had not realized that the very point of the machine was wonder itself.

That is what the clock has done for me. Like a patient God it has taught me to wonder again at the world as I did when

I was a child; before my years of doubt and cynicism; before my dark days.

I went to the theatre in the garden half a dozen times before I summoned the courage to stay behind and introduce myself to Leesa. We went to a café and began a life-conversation. She too is a believer in not knowing. After coffee, she asked me to bring her to the cathedral to show me some of the things about the clock she had not observed on her own visits in the past. There was a bombardment that day. The walls shook from distant detonations as we stood near the sandbags at the base of the clock and then a near explosion threw us together. I drew her to me and pulled us both back into a nook behind the clock. If it fell, I knew it was likely to come away from its anchors and fall forward, and so we huddled there. I was helpless to protect the clock anymore than I already had with the sandbags. If the stupidity of men was about to take the life out of the Wolsenburg clock, and perhaps out of me, there was nothing more I could do. But I could do my best to keep Leesa from getting her brains dashed out by a falling piece of stone.

Huddled there with dust and small bits of debris raining down around me, I embraced not only Leesa, but also uncertainty. I did not know if any of us: me, Leesa, Stimmler, or the clock would survive the day. I see now that it is possible to want to know, and yet to be satisfied, or no, to be thrilled by what I cannot know: the mystery of what happens when we die, why the cat's purr is a gift, the wonder of Leesa welcoming me into her arms as I held her in my own.

The Enlightenment Clock — 1809

By 1771, the wrought-iron gear wheels of the second clock have deteriorated so badly that it stops altogether. The clock itself has become a victim of time at last. It is as if an old soul has expired. Casual observers see simply that the dramatic chimes and automata no longer perform at the appointed hours. Those who know the clock better see at a glance that its dials, including the obvious dial for local time, are no longer accurate. And intimates of the clock, its keepers who have been nursing it through its last days knowing that when its heart stops beating, there is nothing they can do to revive it, those people are aware of the myriad unseen movements now gone still. They are the ones who feel the end most deeply and mourn for what others call "the failure of the mechanism". It is an offensive expression. To operate with relative accuracy for ten generations before faltering is nothing like a failure, especially given that the observations of astronomers have altered perceptions of time in the past two hundred years.

In other ways, the clock continues to be present. There is no discussion whatsoever about removing it from the cathedral. There is talk of repair, but even the great clockmakers of Austria, Germany, France, and even Switzerland suggest that replacing parts would be a fool's occupation. Most admit that it would take them years merely to understand the interconnectedness of the works. So the clock will continue to stand and be esteemed as a monument. The paintings and sculptures will be admired and their meanings puzzled over.

At the very moment that the fixed central disk seizes up an infant is born at an estate in the country nearby. He is the bastard son of Count Beust, the emperor's cousin, and is given the name Jean-Auguste Stimmler.

A dry, attic room, sparse of furniture or possessions. Jean-Auguste's mother, Carina, on the floor, kneeling with her arms on the straw-filled mattress as if saying her bedtime prayers. There is a stick of wood in her mouth which she bites to stifle her cries, and yet animal noises: growls, shrieks, and hisses, slip past the gnawed branch. Jean-Auguste begins to emerge and she squats back further, lowering her planetary stomach and crouching deeper to push him out.

When he is older and legendary, there will be those who swear that at birth he took the midwife's blade, knotted his own umbilical cord and then severed it while the stunned woman looked on in wonder and Carina collapsed on the bed.

As Jean-Auguste grows up, he is precocious and intelligent. By the time he is eight years old, his mother does not know quite what to do with him. She does her best to keep him quiet in polite company, or, better yet, to keep him away from the class of people who are Count Beust's social circle. For the most part, that is fine with him. He dislikes their fancy clothes: the lace and wigs and powder. If he happens to be at work in the garden when guests of the count pass by, he stops work and stands still; better for them to ignore him completely. They do not need to look down upon him. None wish to acknowledge his existence and no one would ever make eye contact with him no matter what he did.

Almost no one.

He knows who his father is and even at his young age, he understands the hypocrisy in Beust's willingness to be intimate with Carina sexually (which will last precisely until her beauty fades) and his unwillingness to so much as glance at her in public.

On Sundays, Jean-Auguste has only to see to the stables and livestock and then he is free for the rest of the day, so by mid-morning he has finished his work and cleaned himself up enough that he is permitted to accompany his mother to mass at the cathedral in the city. There are country churches close by which are regularly attended by the population of the estate, but on holidays, Beust allows his carriages and carts to be harnessed as transportation to the great Wolsenburg cathedral so his servants may celebrate in style. The cathedral, after centuries, is still one of the tallest and most grand buildings in Europe.

It is Easter, so when Jean-Auguste and his mother arrive at the cathedral square, it is full of people who have traveled from around the countryside to be at mass. The sun stretches long arms across the cobbles but the monolith of the cathedral keeps half of the square in shadow so to stand in one place is to be chilled by spring air, and to stand in another is to allow the skin a taste of the summer still to come. They have arrived well before the next service is due to begin; the humble clock on the tower of the municipal hall tells them so.

Jean-Auguste wanders into the building, leaning his head back to marvel at the sheer height of the bell tower as he enters. He walks up the southern aisle and into the right arm of the transept where the stilled clock stands. As he is admiring it, he happens to overhear a cleric talking with a visitor to the Wolsenburg cathedral. The cleric tells the visitor about the clock and says that though it has remained as a remarkable example of the art of the renaissance in Wolsenburg, it is a shame that the clock will never be made to work again.

Jean-Auguste has been standing behind the pillar of the angels, which is decorated with life-sized statues. He pipes up from behind the column and announces that indeed the clock can be made to work again and that he is the one who will do it.

The visitor and the cleric think one of the angels is speaking to them.

At the estate, there is an enclosed, formal garden. It is fenced to keep out deer and rabbits and the north entrance, nearest the main house, is a large, green, wooden door. Unless the count's estate is full of guests (it is often full of guests), Jean is permitted free access to all the grounds when he is finished his chores.

The garden is one of his favourite places. The fence might keep out fauna but it does little to contain Jean-Auguste's imagination. His mind blossoms with ideas and although he often forgets to eat despite his growing body, he is starving with curiosity about everything around him.

Many of the elements of the garden have been adapted from André Le Nôtre's plans of the famous gardens in Versailles, so there are allées of beech and ash with hidden fountains, a labyrinth ending at an ornate belvedere, geometric garden beds, and, most astonishingly, hydraulic automata. One fountain is a statue of King Neptune who has a perpetual procession of dolphins leaping over his lap. Another is a water joke which is a statue of Daphne surrounded by a laurel tree. As the statue is nowhere near a pond or fountain, it is a great surprise to unwary visitors when they pass by and jets of water squirt out of Daphne's breasts.

To swing back the green door on a spring morning, is to open a dreamscape and walk inside. Jean-Auguste presses the latch, pushes open the door, steps in and closes the door behind him. His brain has memorized the patterns of the garden. He has done all he can to trace his way back into the imagination of the planner and into the mind of the engineer who has created the fountains. He is as protective of the garden as the head gardener and has developed an enthusiastic taste for venison and rabbit, thanks to his proclivity for conservation.

He is ten years old and knows that the summer will be his last taste of something like freedom before he is sent to earn his keep as a clerk or apprentice somewhere.

Thanks to Count Beust's library and the patience and kindness of the governess who is the instructor of the count's legitimate children, Jean-Auguste has learned to read and has studied mathematics. He steals into the garden, carrying under his arm a recent treatise on perception by Johann Wolfgang von Goethe, borrowed from the reading room when no one was looking.

As he rounds a corner looking for a quiet place to hide and read for a few hours (he knows he can disappear for most of the morning without being missed — the eggs have been collected and the horses have been tended to) he sees the count fucking his mother in an ivy-covered alcove.

Beust is fully clothed but his breeches are pulled down so what dominates the image is his white ass pumping in just the same way and with the same speed as Butsa, the count's great Pyrenee, mounts a bitch.

Carina is lifted on a stone ledge. Her petticoats are pushed around her waist and Jean can see her bare thighs meeting Beust's frantic motions. Beust has his right hand cupped firmly over her mouth and his left is a fist tearing at her gown as he forces her against the wall.

When Jean's mother sees him, her eyes open wide, but, trapped as she is, there is little she can do even to alert Count Beust to her son's presence.

Goethe's theory of perception is that it rests within the mind, so that to perceive as fortunate or unfortunate the nearby presence of the gardener's pitchfork, depends on the state of mind of the observer. For Jean-Auguste, the pitchfork is both fortunate and unfortunate at once. He extracts it from its bale of weeds and brings the sharp tines in contact with Count Beust's powdered buttocks. Blood springs forth in very much the manner of the water from Daphne's breasts, and the count howls with surprise very much in the manner of Butsa moaning his surprise at the full moon.

It is an end and a beginning.

The incident marks the end of Jean-Auguste's freedom in the garden and the beginning of his apprenticeship. It also marks the end of Count Beust's sexual trysts with his servants and the beginning of a rather long convalescence in which he needs to invent excuses for his inability to sit, ride his horse, or dance with his wife at formal occasions.

Carina is permitted to remain in the employ of Count Beust on the condition that Jean-Auguste be sent away to work. It is a concession. Sent on her own way, Carina would have few options and to remain at the estate means that she will have some slight advantage over the count in that she could easily cause a scandal. Beust feels himself in a precarious position; he clearly is not safe around his illegitimate son, and yet the boy is his own blood and he has some responsibility for him and thinks that finding a way to provide for him at a distance will create peace all around.

Beust finds him work with a bookbinder in Paris. With the boy there, the count honours his quiet obligations and also keeps Jean-Auguste away so he does not have to watch his back, not that he has much opportunity, for several months, to think about anything but his back.

The bookbinder is Pieter Guilebert and he has a building east of Montmartre, just outside the city limits so he may avoid paying municipal taxes. Count Beust has arranged for Jean-Auguste's transportation to Guilebert's shop to be as uncomfortable as possible, so Jean-Auguste arrives with a sore backside from the carriage ride from Wolsenburg, and sore legs from the ten kilometer walk the rest of the way from the carriage's destination in Paris to Guilebert's. Despite his discomfort, he is aware that he is nowhere near as sore as his father and this knowledge makes the voyage quite bearable.

When he arrives, it is pouring rain. Jean-Auguste carries a sack with the extra shirt he owns, two books stolen from the library at the estate, and a letter of introduction from Count Beust. It is mid-morning. He knocks on Guilebert's door feeling some trepidation at what the new circumstances of his life are to be but also recognizing his enthusiasm for being close to a city like Paris and for the chance to learn new things.

As the door opens, a cascade of rain spills out from the eaves and over Jean-Auguste's head. Guilebert's housekeeper peeks out and asks him what his business is. However, she asks in French and Jean-Auguste does not understand. She thinks perhaps he is an idiot beggar and begins to close the door but he slides his foot across the threshold giving him time to remove the letter from the sack and hand it to her. She reads it and rolls her eyes and says to him, still in French, "Lovely then, another charge of Count Beust's, which means another child-minding job for me. Come in, come in then. If you plan to make yourself ill be sure you get sick enough to die quickly. Monsieur Guilebert does not pay me enough to tend to unhealthy bastards."

Jean-Auguste blinks his eyes, takes off his soaked cap, and bows genially toward the maid.

"Don't stand there bowing," she says, "come through to the bindery and meet the master. Lucky for you, business is good. You look thin and you seem rather stupid, but I'm sure there will be some work for you so long as you are co-ordinated enough to use a needle and thread."

In the bindery, Guilebert is whacking one of his employees over the head with a thick piece of leather and is yelling at the top of his lungs in high German, which is the language Jean-Auguste has been brought up with. Guilebert is a handsome man, thin and very well-dressed. Jean-Auguste can see that he is not someone who dirties his hands in his own shop. His nose is long and rather pointed. He wears a short-cropped wig and an embroidered waistcoat under his wool jacket. He thinks his employees have no respect for him and believes they mock him behind his back at every opportunity. He knows he pays them a reasonable wage, certainly comparable with other bookbinderies. Let them try to find better employment close by. No one who works for him is starving, and if they are, it is because they drain all of their pay onto the wall behind Le Fin Du Monde in the evenings, so they are slow and inefficient in the morning when they come to work.

The man Guilebert hits is responsible for incorrectly collating three hundred copies of the new novel by Pierre Ambroise François Choder los de Laclos titled *Les Liaisons Dangereuses*, so now the books must all be taken apart, the signatures must be reassembled in the correct order, and the copies must be sewn again. Some, no doubt, will be ruined, and as Guilebert knows he is unlikely to be able to extract recompense from his employee, he feels justified in at least using the man as a release for several months' worth of frustration, which, in Guilebert's case, is a considerable amount of ire.

The other labourers, used to Guilebert's outbursts, continue in their work. Jean-Auguste and the housekeeper wait. When the beating is over, Guilebert glances up and sees the pair watching him from the doorway. He sets the strop down on a counter and with it sets his ill humour. He has had the pleasure of vigorous physical activity, why go on being angry?

Jean-Auguste meets his eyes as he approaches. Guilebert says hello and the housekeeper steps in front of Jean-Auguste to hand Guilebert the letter from Count Beust. "He's another 'little secret' from the count, sir," she says. "I think he's rather thick and cannot speak. He hasn't said a word, just handed me this letter and stood there dripping wet until I brought him here. He seems sickly and I need you to know that I do not have time to play nurse so I say send him home and let the count feed and clothe the poor boy. Even if he does speak, he won't be speaking the same language as the rest here and what good will that do? Turn him loose sir, now before he can call this his home. What do you owe

Count Beust that would make this taking on of his own duties worthwhile to you?"

"I fail to see how any of that might be your concern, Marianne," Guilbert says as he finishes reading the letter, "but I will allow myself to ignore your impertinence because I do understand that your duties will include the care of this boy. So I can tell you that the question is not 'What do I owe Count Beust?' but 'What does he now owe me?' In my mind, that is a much more interesting question."

Jean-Auguste steps out from behind the housekeeper, who startles and pushes him behind her, so he bounds in front again with an odd, eighteenth-century square dance move, quickly bows and, using the French he has picked up in the past fifteen minutes says, "*Bonjour* Monsieur Guilebert. *Excusez mon impertinence. Je suis mince, mais j'nais pas stupide. Chanceux pour vous les affaires sont bonnes.*"

"Ah, very impressive, boy," Guilebert says in German. "The count's letter says you speak only German. How is it that you come to greet me in French?"

"I have learned a little bit recently, and before long I will be fluent," Jean-Auguste says, this time in German. "Excuse me if you will for being presumptuous, sir, but I see a dozen men here tooling by hand the identical design on the covers of these books. Would it not be more efficient and more consistent to have a machine that would do this work for you?"

He is indeed presumptuous, but Guilebert likes the child already. He seems fearless and his eyes burn with a real curiosity that Guilebert recognizes as a glow he has seen in brilliant men. "A machine! Ah, yes, would that not be wonderful! But then, why not simply make a machine that would allow me to stamp my own francs so I would no longer need to have these men toil over their work so?"

"The process would be very similar, I imagine, but I suspect the government would have more to say about you producing your own coins than about you becoming a maker of books known all around the world. So let us begin with the engravings in the leather first and move on from there as we are ready."

Guilebert can not tell if the boy is serious or not. He has a very earnest face. Either way, for the first time in years, Guilebert has been knocked off his guard, and for the first time ever, including his own childhood, it is a ten-year-old boy who has set him back.

Jean-Auguste works in the bindery for seven years. Since he cares little for creature comforts, he negotiates with Guilebert to be paid only half-salary in return for unlimited access to bindery books, an unlimited supply of paper for note taking, and an unlimited supply of candles to light his room. Guilebert agrees hastily and later regrets it. The boy learns to read French fluently in just a few months and sleeps only four or five hours a night. His tiny room under the rafters is jammed full of books. He takes a dozen or more every week. He almost never goes out with his fellows and yet they seem to like him anyway. And worse, as far as the master can tell, because Jean-Auguste does not drink or socialize, he manages, to Guilebert's horror, to squirrel away most of his wages.

He reads everything he can about science and is fascinated by electricity, mechanics, and especially medicine and anatomy. It is a heady time of innovation and many of the new discoveries and new approaches to old things Jean-Auguste reads about seem like magic to him. He understands things intellectually, and yet that does not take away the wonder of the emerging marvels around him.

One of the monographs that comes in to the bindery is a small book called *Inventum Novum, or A New Discovery that Enables the Physician from the Percussion of the Human Thorax to Detect the Diseases Hidden Within the Chest,* by Dr. Leopold Auenbrugger of Vienna. Of particular interest to Jean-Auguste are Auenbrugger's post-mortem studies in which he has conducted autopsies in order to verify the diagnoses made while the patient was alive.

Without any formal medical training, Jean-Auguste has developed a theory. He believes sounds within the human body provide a myriad of diagnostic possibilities and he has been working on a model for an instrument which will allow doctors to better hear the heartbeat and respiratory functions.

And so it is difficult to know what to name the circumstance which next irrevocably alters Jean-Auguste's life: coincidence, serendipity, or God's will.

He makes the trip into Paris infrequently. He has attended mass at Notre Dame but was less impressed with the structure than some of his fellow worshippers because he has, from a very young age had the opportunity to pray at the Wolsenburg cathedral, which in his mind is every bit as grand.

The men he works with come into the city for leisure because they prefer to drink and fornicate away from their families and merely suffer the consequences of their debauchery when they go back home. For his part, Jean-Auguste helps them treat the infections they pick up on these sojourns, which both maintains his popularity and keeps the others from teasing him when he attends lectures at the Hotel-Dieu instead of accompanying them to the brothel. Not that he has avoided the brothel altogether. His curiosity and his chemistry lead him there when he is fourteen, and he visits on one or two other occasions, but he has read about some of the most unseemly diseases that can result from promiscuity, and the truth is he simply hasn't the time for it.

That is how he comes to be sitting in the lecture theatre at the Hotel-Dieu one spring day in 1788 when Dr. Auenbrugger steps on stage and begins to speak.

After the lecture, Jean-Auguste approaches Dr. Auenbrugger. Jean-Auguste is surrounded by a cloud of flying paper. He perpetually carries with him a satchel of notes which he adds to when inspiration strikes him. Since inspiration strikes him more often than Guielbert strikes his employees, Jean-Auguste has rather a mass of notes. He is searching for his drawings of the machine which will help doctors listen to the organs of their patients, and becomes more and more frantic as he digs in his bag. The doctor turns his attention to Jean-Auguste. He is exceedingly calm. He looks at Jean-Auguste with a patient eye.

"Herr Doctor," Jean-Auguste says, "I have been fascinated by your work. I have read your book. I have . . . notes,
here, somewhere. An idea. An idea for listening."

Leopold Auenbrugger listens.

"Your thoughts about percussion, you see, led me to think
about the sounds the organs make naturally: the rush of air
into the lungs, the beating of the heart and how wonderful
it would be to amplify those sounds for diagnosis. Ah, here,
you see. Here is a drawing." Jean-Auguste is breathless and
hunches over to try to recover his wind.

Leopold studies the drawing for a few moments. He hums
and nods. Then he snaps his wrist and hands the paper back
to Jean-Auguste. "This is your work, my boy?" he asks.

"No other, sir. I know you may have reason to doubt me. I
have not studied at the university and I have no credentials,
but I have read everything I could get my hands on since I
was five years old . . . "

"Including my book."

"Yes, especially your book, in fact."

"Are you employed?"

"Yes, I work for a bookbinder outside of the city. There
would have been no better vocation for me. Other than,
perhaps, librarian."

"Have you any idea what is happening here in Paris right
now?"

"Oh, everything, from what I can tell. There are men like
you everywhere and . . . "

"Yes, yes, I can see you are excited about the age, my boy.
What is your name?"

"I am Jean-Auguste Stimmler, at your service, sir."

"Well, Jean-Auguste Stimmler, my valet has refused to return to Vienna with me and I must leave immediately so if you would really like to be at my service, I need a new valet and an assistant. I can see that you are very much a citizen of the mind but I'm afraid that may not be enough to allow you to survive what many of us can see is about to happen here in Paris."

"What is it that you see, sir?"

"Simply this my young friend: the world is about to end."

As the revolution rages in France, Jean-Auguste begins his career with Dr. Auenbrugger. There are rumours that the clergy and the nobility in France have united to collect all the nation's grain and ship it away to starve the people. In the summer, revolutionaries attack the Bastille prison and blood begins to flow in the streets of Paris.

Leopold and Jean-Auguste are safely ensconced in Vienna at the medical school where the doctor continues his research. Here, they work together for two years on the corpses the university has procured for Leopold. Most of the bodies used for dissection are criminals who have been put to death. It is best when the specimen has been hanged, but sometimes they get a body that has been guillotined. In such cases, the head is usually, but not always, returned with the rest of the corpse and, as Leopold's studies primarily involve the region of the thorax, Jean-Auguste is permitted to examine the severed heads as much as he pleases. He is very interested in the intricacies of the body as concentrated in the neck just at the place where it is severed. The respiratory system, the circulatory system, and the nervous system, all travel through the small channel of the neck as if it were a vital passage between worlds.

There is a kind of glee Jean-Auguste feels working with the Doctor. He loves the practice of tangible study, loves tracing the line of an artery from the heart around a lung and under a shoulder where it disappears, and yet it is the more basic processes that fascinate him most.

He loves hands and feet. The totality of bones and ligaments and tendons that allow humans to do so many wonderful and horrible things, are a marvel. He can see from a small nub of bone on a finger, that this person was a scribe, or from the evidence of repeated fractures and healing in the digits, that this person was a labourer, likely a farm worker used to abusing his hands in his efforts. It is the interconnectedness of the tissues that impresses him. Dr. Auenbrugger fosters his interests by allowing him to do what work he likes on the bodies in his own time. In the months that Jean-Auguste has been with him, Leopold has recognized what an extraordinary young man he is. He has an excellent intellect and an original mind. In truth, Leopold can see that he will easily be surpassed by his pupil; no small feat since there are those in Europe who believe that Auenbrugger is the most distinguished physician alive. If his ego were bigger, he would be threatened by the boy.

Instead, he is threatened by a pounding on the door late one evening while he and Jean-Auguste are at work. There is no prohibition against human dissection. However, as medicine advances, the corpses of executed criminals are in greater demand and so medical schools have become less stringent about where cadavers for study have been obtained. A local woman has recently died and shortly thereafter, the family has been given the news that her remains have been plundered by grave robbers. At the cemetery, their worst fears have been confirmed; the grave has been exhumed, the casket opened and the body removed. The family has collected a small mob of angry supporters and they have stormed the university looking for their lost mother and for vindication.

The pounding on the door has been coming from a nurse who in turn has been told that there is an angry mob at the gate there to retrieve their matron's body.

"We haven't got any women here," Leopold tells her. "Ask them to go home."

"Wait a minute," Jean-Auguste says, "there is one."

"Which one?"

"This one. The lungs."

"Well, yes, all right, we do have one woman, but we've had her for months now."

"What shall I tell the crowd, Doctor?"

"Tell them the truth as I've told it to you. We haven't got any women here but one, and they're welcome to her if that will make them happy."

"But you would do well to mention that she is flayed open like a butterfly at the moment," Jean-Auguste says. "And by the way, Leopold, she was guillotined and we haven't got her head."

"Hmm, that might make things interesting, might it not? There is a way out through the sewers. Let us go quickly."

"Doctor?" the nurse says.

"Come with us," Leopold says. "They will not leave without their corpse, and since we haven't the one they are seeking, I'm afraid they might be inclined to make a corpse out of you."

Zala, the nurse, is just twenty years old, the same age as Jean-Auguste, but she has worked in the hospital building since she was twelve, so it is she who leads the two men out to safety.

As they make their escape, they hear glass shatter. The laboratory is ransacked. Leopold steps more quickly as the gravity of the problem becomes tangible to him. The leather of his shoes is befouled by the water in the passageway but his mind is singly focussed on escape.

The doctor does not feel that returning to his home will be safe, so Zala takes them to the apartment she lives in with her mother and father and four siblings. The parents are honoured to have the medical men in their home, but when they discover the reason for their visit, they become anxious, not merely because they fear the arrival of an angry mob, but because they are not certain how to feel about having in their home men who desecrate the dead.

The family shifts children around so that Leopold and Jean-Auguste may have a room of their own, and Zala brings bread and cheese and wine for their nourishment. Neither man has taken notice of her before, but in this new context, Jean-Auguste finds himself admiring her. She is rather beautiful and he wonders why he has not noticed her before. Then he realizes that at work at the medical building, she must have been near him often. Here in her home, she has been looking at him and he at her. He has noted the flecks of green in her brown eyes. There, however, she did not meet his gaze. In Count Beust's garden, the gentry had not so much as glanced in his direction and such unseeing has been his relationship with Zala. Now, he has become one of those people who, as a sign of respect, should not be looked at directly. He feels he has not changed at all inside himself, but sees that his relationship with the doctor is all that it has taken to move him up a notch in the class structure. Since he has seen the negative effect of class on people like his mother, he is distressed by this revelation and immediately moves to change it.

When Zala puts down the food on the table and turns to leave, he reaches out and touches her arm lightly. "Will you not stay and take a glass of wine with us? Surely your spirits are as elevated as ours and you will not sleep too quickly tonight."

He expects that she will hesitate and offer regrets, or that she will thank him but politely refuse. Instead, she straightens her skirt around her waist and says, "I do not often take a drink, Herr Stimmler, but tonight, yes, a small, medicinal draught might do. Allow me to fetch another glass."

She leaves the room and returns so quickly that Jean-Auguste can only assume that the glass was just outside the door all along. She must have brought it with the meal and left it on the table outside the door before she entered. He pours her half a glass of wine. It is white wine and has been kept so cool somewhere that it produces an opaque frost on the outside of the glass. "I think perhaps a stronger dose might be in order tonight," she says, and he fills the glass to the top.

They talk about the mob and the problem Dr. Auenbrugger will have continuing his work. Zala astonishes Jean-Auguste with her insights. It is as though the three of them have been working together for months. In a way, they have been. Zala has been cleaning tools and equipment and has come and gone along with several other nurses and Jean-Auguste continues to feel embarrassment realizing that in his concentration and his ignorance, he has treated her with little respect all this time.

Leopold is shaken. "I cannot see any other possibility," he says, "I will have to leave the university and take up a post elsewhere to continue."

"But your studies have been innocent. You have not stolen any bodies," Zala says.

"And yet they have been taken for exactly the use that we put them toward. How can we be sure the bodies we have been cutting up have been given freely?" Jean-Auguste asks.

"Because I would not take a cadaver without knowing its origins. Good Lord, there are enough corpses being produced by the Revolution to keep a thousand schools supplied without question, and death is not unknown here in Vienna." But Leopold knows the truth: that most of those executed in France are not criminals, not by any reasonable measure. This fact, more than the angry crowd, is what has him rattled. He has not wanted to examine his morals too closely and now that he has no choice, he finds the self-realizations uncomfortable. It is a night for uneasy self-reflection.

"I may be able to make contact with colleagues in Munich. We might be safe there. If we could find a way to hide ourselves in a carriage until we are out of the city, we should be able to flee safely," Leopold says. "That crowd was but the first. More will come. We will not be able to work as freely as in the past. Perhaps the hospital will also run us out."

"Or, we will have to come up with something else," Jean-Auguste says.

"Another supply of criminals?"

"Another way of studying the body altogether."

"How do you propose to do that, my young friend? Shall we start farms for the purpose?"

"It is a practical suggestion, given the number of unwanted children in the world," Zala says, "but I think that should not be any more popular than the theft of the dead."

"No, no," Jean-Auguste says, "must I be the one to teach you both how to think? If our trouble comes from taking apart dead bodies to understand how they work, then perhaps we should approach the problem from a different direction. Rather than dissecting the dead, we should begin at the beginning and put together a body to see how it works. Let us not look at life after it is over. Let us make a being ourselves and bring it to life. Let us create and give a breath of life to something dead."

"Jean-Auguste, I have known you as a brilliant and humble student, and now you surprise me with the claim that you would like to do what only God can accomplish. Is it not a kind of sacrilege?" Leopold says.

"I do not wish to *be* God," Jean-Auguste says, "I merely wish to get a little nearer to understanding how he *thinks*."

Leopold considers Jean-Auguste's idea over the next few weeks, but he believes that the proposal is impractical. It is not that he doubts his young assistant's abilities; if he says he will build a human being, then he will. But Auenbrugger thinks it will take him a lifetime or two and the doctor hasn't the time to spare. He will return to his home city of Graz, where, for a while at least, it will be possible to simply pick up where he left off and continue his research. That means that he and Jean-Auguste will part ways and that Leopold will not be able to give him much assistance.

Auenbrugger is surprised at the amount of money Jean-Auguste has at his disposal and at first he wonders what kind of thievery his friend (for that is what they have become) has been up to in order to arrange the finances he has set in order, but Jean-Auguste assures him that all of his resources have been acquired legally, through abstinence more than anything else.

In fact, his wealth is modest but it is enough to rent a small workshop in Vienna for a year and to feed himself and, most importantly, to buy the supplies he needs.

He asks Zala to leave the medical school and work with him. Anyone else might be offended by the nature of his proposal, but she has come to know him well in the short time they have spent time together. He says, "I cannot afford to pay you as an assistant, but I do need your help. I will keep you fed and clothed and I am quite good at taking care of people when they are ill."

"You are quite good at taking care of them when they are dead," she says. "I've seen the buckets full of parts."

"No longer," he says. "Now, where was I?"

"Taking care of the dead."

"No, no, taking care of you. I propose that we marry so that I might . . . well, take care of you. Yes."

"Did you provide my answer for me, or was that 'yes' a way of you affirming that you'd got your own question right?"

"Marriage. I was proposing. To you . . . Did I not? . . . Just now?"

"Yes."

"Yes I did, or yes you will?"

"Both," she says, "but let us be clear from the start. I think I shall be the one taking care of you."

Jean-Auguste begins, wisely, with a mechanical child rather than an adult model. In fact, he begins with the arms. His aim is to produce fingers that will wiggle and ball up into fists. For this purpose, he fabricates small rods which mimic the bones of a human hand. There are 73 rods in each hand. In order for the parts of his creation to move, he needs a motor which can be wound to provide energy, and to learn more about motors, he buys three expensive clocks and disassembles them.

"I thought there were to be no more dissections," Zala says.

"This is different."

"In what way is it different, dearest? There are clock parts from one end of the room to the other."

"Because I will put these back together. And they will chime again. You will see."

Within a week, his promise has come true. All three clocks have been restored and he has even improved on them. At midnight, the newly amplified chimes drive Zala nearly insane.

After nine months, the infant has taken on a relatively mortal shape. Jean-Auguste has toyed with the idea of simply using a doll's head, but he wants more authenticity so he carves one himself out of wood. He has been struggling over a way to reproduce the movement of the lips and to find a material which will, like a human throat, convey milk to a chamber where his child will digest it and then convey it further for excretion.

Leopold, understanding instantly its potential use to Jean-Auguste, has sent him a report by Charles Marie de la Condamine about cautchouc which has been discovered along the Amazon river, and after obtaining a sample of the material, Jean-Auguste has produced a rubber hose for his purposes. He is not the first to make this discovery, but he makes it independently of others in Europe who have worked with this new substance.

Now, a year has gone by and the infant is far from finished. What Jean-Auguste has accomplished is miraculous. The baby resembles a too-young cadaver, wearing a long white dress splayed open at the front so Jean-Auguste can get at the interior works. Its feet stick out from the bottom of the gown and, when tickled, the baby coos, and wiggles its arms and shoulders.

But he is out of funds and out of materials. He has months, perhaps years worth of work still to do and no means to accomplish it.

Zala brings coffee in the middle of the afternoon and, as is their custom, he leaves his worktable and sits with her near the window for half an hour or so.

"Woebegauer let me have these apple cakes for free this morning. He says I am only just now starting to get some flesh on me and I've been eating his baking for a year. I shall be a bad example for his other patrons if I do not begin to eat more, he says."

"Then here is to Woebegauer for providing," Jean-Auguste says. He means no malice by it, but Zala knows they are out of money. Still, he feels it is important to say what both of them have recognized weeks ago, "I have failed, Zala. The Little Patient is not finished and I haven't the money to continue. I will have to find employment somewhere and I will have to give up my project. I have been thinking about writing to Dr. Auenbrugger to see if he will take me back as an assistant."

"You are hardly a failure, Jean-Auguste. You have learned more from what you have done in the last twelve months than Leopold has learned in his lifetime. I think he would tell you so. You must think of another way. That has been your greatest strength."

"Your faith in me is important, do not think it is not, but I think I may have been defeated this time."

"Perhaps, but I am not so willing to give up yet. I thought that it was an irony that you could not finish your Little Patient, but now I see that it may well simply be a sign. It may be that there are other things you need to apply your mind to. I do not know what, but I'm certain that I will find out soon."

"What do you mean 'an irony'?"

"I mean that you have spent a year of your life trying to build yourself a baby, and without much effort at all, you made one in the course of a night sometime last month."

In the thirteen years since he was sent away, Jean-Auguste has twice visited his mother on Count Beust's estate. Carina was merely sixteen when her son was born, so she is now thirty-nine, but looks closer to fifty thanks to years of service in Beust's kitchen.

More than half of his life has been lived without her, and yet Jean-Auguste feels an easy love for her. He knows that there was no choice but for them to be separated when he was a child, and he knows that they have both lived better than they would have otherwise because of it. He cannot help feeling the loss that comes along with the sudden recognition that as the years wore on, it was not so much she who abandoned him, but he who abandoned her. When he sees her, it is as if his heart clenches and it pains him. He vows silently that he will not leave again without her.

Count Beust receives Jean-Auguste, appropriately, in his library. The count has also aged. It is not an easy time for the aristocracy in Europe. France has executed King Louis XVI and Marie Antoinette, annexed Belgium, and declared war on Austria and Prussia, and then also on Britain, Holland, and Spain. Nobles across the continent have become contrite or obstinate. Beust is a mixture of both. At least now he is willing to look Jean-Auguste in the eye.

Beust sits behind his writing table holding the reservoir pen he has been using. It is a rare invention and a practical one; it does away with the labour involved in cutting and trimming quill pens, which many people, including Jean-Auguste, still use. He plans to exhibit a demeanour of industry toward Jean-Auguste, so that he might be rid of him as quickly as possible.

A manservant Jean-Auguste does not recognize, shows him into the room, backs out, and closes the doors behind him, leaving the two of them alone.

Beust pretends to finish a letter. He glances up, then turns his attention back to his sheet of paper and says, "You have done well for yourself, I am told. It is indeed a new world when a boy like you may rise in the ranks of society."

"It *is* a new world. Men fly about in balloons, steam engines weave cloth, bastards work at universities, and kings lose their heads. One wonders what might come next," he says. Then, taking Beust's measure, he adds, "Father."

Beust sets down the pen and gives Jean-Auguste his attention. "You come to me for a reason, I presume? Perhaps you would care to add your name to the list of those wishing to extort funds from me?"

"It is true that at some time in the past, I have thought that one day I might betray the secret of my origins, or threaten you with scandal by asserting my parentage, but, if I may speak frankly, I do not suppose that the simple realization

that I am your bastard son would create notice in society, let
alone a scandal. In fact, drawing attention to the circumstance that you are my father is more likely to damage my
reputation than yours, I believe."

"You are impertinent and offensive, boy," Beust slouches
back in his chair and rubs his forehead, "but I have become
too old to rage against it. And, at any rate, you speak the
truth, so I have little ground for objection. Still, there must
be some purpose in your visitation other than to mock me.
What is it you have come here for?"

"Money, as you suppose, but I merely want a loan . . . no,
an investment, which I will pay back double within two years."

"It is a foolish banker who believes the claims of the
destitute when they say they can produce great riches. How
is it that you propose to increase my . . . investment so?"

"You have seen exhibits of automata; those moving dolls
that astonish people with their acrobatic movements, or
mechanical birds in cages that appear to sing. I know that
you have here at the estate a snuff box with a working model
of a knife-grinder's workshop under the lid which is a great
joy to you."

"True, I have a weakness for these toys and they have
always delighted me. What is your part in it?"

"I have been involved in a year long study in which I
plan to make a mechanical model of life — a mechanical
human being that is like any other man. But I recognize it
is a lofty aim and a goal that will not be achieved easily. In
the meantime, I propose to take some of the skills I have
acquired and apply them to a new breed of automata which

will astound audiences around the globe and which will easily earn their keep by the turn of a mechanical key."

Beust can see the passion in Jean-Auguste's eyes and he feels himself strangely compelled by the argument. He also feels something else welling up inside him. His legitimate sons are, he admits, lazy idiots who spend all of their time frittering away his money planning one festivity after another. Yet here is a boy, his own blood whether he likes it or not, who clearly has gifts beyond his station in life. Beust feels something he has never felt before, and though he does not quite recognize it, what the feeling is, is pride.

"Imagine," Jean-Auguste continues, "if I could build you a model that could sit at your desk, just as you sit there now, a model that could hold your intricate reservoir pen and write a letter for you. I could make him write anything you like. I could even have him draw a writ of indenture. The automata I have seen in Paris and Vienna are mere toys compared to what I want to do. I know audiences would pay richly to see them and that I could attract the attention of the most powerful men. Let us set our history aside, Count Beust, and see ourselves as two men who are making a business agreement. Nothing more."

Beust considers Jean-Auguste's proposal. Like many other men Jean-Auguste has encountered, Beust has been caught unaware and set off his guard. "What, exactly, do you need?" he asks.

"A workshop, a stipend for living expenses and supplies . . . "

"For how long?"

"I have plans drawn for the first model. With time and resources, I could build it within half a year. But there is one more thing I require."

"What is that?"

"I need you to release my mother from her obligations to you."

"That is no small list, Jean-Auguste," Beust says. It is the first time he has called his son by name, "If we are to, as you say, cast off history and be two men of business, then I shall have no more responsibility for you or your mother; instead, you will be obliged to me."

The first automata he builds is a flute player. When it is finished, there is nothing like it in the world. Spectators think the sound must be coming from a pipe organ in the pedestal of the device, but when they inspect it closely, they can see that the player is indeed playing the flute.

Zala is well acquainted with the workings of the player because Jean-Auguste has made her learn the flute so that he could study the intricacies of the art.

The flute player is four feet tall, and can play twelve different tunes, each of which require a different music cylinder to be inserted. He blows air through his lips producing pressure in varying degrees to achieve different octaves, and his fingers move over the flute holes to produce distinct notes. Several fingers move at the same time, the lips purse and open, and the player moves his mouth in front of and behind the mouthpiece and also raises and lowers the instrument as a live flute player would. There are eight bellows inside which provide the varying degrees of air pressure required and a crankshaft that manipulates the movement of the fingers according to the tune programmed on the cylinder.

Jean-Auguste presents his Flute Player at the re-established National Institute of Science along with two other inventions: the Goose, and the Writer.

The Writer is a boy three feet high and seated at a desk with an inkwell on the right, a quill pen in his hand, and a sheet of paper in front of him on the table. When his mechanism is engaged, he moves his arm to dip his pen in the inkwell, shakes it, and writes, lifting the pen between words, moving down a line when he gets to the end of the paper, and dotting a full stop at the end of his sentence. His head and his eyes move to follow his task and when he has completed his letter, he gazes up mischievously at the observer with an unnerving gaze which dares them to come and inspect his note.

The Goose is perhaps the most lifelike of Jean-Auguste's creations. When its mechanism is engaged by the stroke of a feather in the neck of the bird, the goose raises its head, then stretches its neck to full extension and flaps its wings and shakes its tail as though emerging from a sleep, honking and snorting as if it might, at any moment, prepare to fly off. Instead, it leans over to a plate which has been supplied with oats and it pecks and eats exactly as a goose in the stableyard might. It lifts its neck and swallows, then continues to consume the grain and, a few moments after it finishes ingesting the meal, the bird defecates on its pedestal, producing not only a mess that must be wiped clean after each performance but a stench which fills the room in a most convincing way.

Nothing he has learned, nothing he has read, nothing he has seen in his lifetime has prepared him for the experience of fatherhood.

While he is working on the Flute Player, Zala grows more obviously pregnant, and he studies each change in her body. He listens endlessly to her abdomen, and to her heart and lungs with the thoraphone he has perfected since he first proposed it to Leopold Auenbrugger.

The birth of his daughter sends him into a deep reverie. Out of nothing, a life! Two bodies stirred together, sperm sloshed about in the chamber of the womb for a short while and the result is this: life!

In the same way that the people who come to look at his machines will marvel at his work, he marvels at the work of God. What other explanation can there be for life, after all? Jean-Auguste is a scientist and an engineer. He understands probabilities and the interrelationship of systems. He does not think that it is possible that humanity could exist without a divine force of some kind nudging the accident of their existence into being.

He has tried to mimic the simplest human movements and has only been humbled by his efforts. When others walk by the sea, pick up a stone and throw it with some accuracy at a log floating on the waves, they take their body's abilities for granted. Jean-Auguste increasingly sees each such gesture as a miracle.

And yet he is undeterred.

Jean-Auguste's devices are so lifelike that people demand he open the cabinets and show them the mechanisms so that they will be convinced there is not some trick, perhaps a child or small person inside the boxes making all the movements themselves.

To his surprise, revealing the works increases the amazement of his spectators, rather than reducing it. To him, the automata are puzzles he has solved, and not always to his satisfaction. There was no fabric he could find, for example, with which to dress the Flute Player's fingers so that they would properly cover the holes of the flute when he was playing, and Jean-Auguste has had to compromise himself and use human skin on the fingers so that it would work.

To him, the mechanisms are the logical working out of engineering principles which are solved by mathematics, physics, and occasional good luck. His goal has long been to produce life in a way that the complexities he must find his way through would be as great as the elaborate human mechanisms he studied with Leopold. He is beginning to see that he has acquired great skill over the years and what to his mind are relatively straightforward devices are miraculous to others. Including other scientists, inventors, and engineers.

As years go by, Jean-Auguste and Zala have more children and he never tires of watching them feed at her breast and from that suckling, grow into walking, talking, demanding beings.

As his family grows, so too does his skill, and he builds more and more complicated and fantastic machines. His sense of humour is exercised as well. Cooks drink too much wine and stumble only to mistakenly release uncooked rabbits from their pots, a magician levitates his assistant and passes a hoop impossibly over the entire length of her body, a trapeze artist walks a tightrope balancing a delicate china cup on his nose.

No one knows how he does it and his fame spreads all across the continent. In the following decades, he is welcomed at court in several countries and his automata regularly perform for royalty and even for the pope. His creations ignite wonder and after a performance he recognizes in the eyes of his audience the look he knows he wears when he looks at Zala and at each one of his children.

It is the admission against his own humility that he is able to inspire people which opens up the possibility for him to begin to pursue his masterpiece, the Wolsenburg Clock.

His devotion is layered. It is 1808 and he is an important man in Wolsenburg. Known around the globe for his inventions, Jean-Auguste Stimmler has entertained orphans and princes alike and has made himself wealthy. In the course of building more and more sophisticated automata, he has had to pioneer materials and design new machines to fabricate the specialized parts he has required. Some of these inventions have used principles which have become the basis for other inventors who have made engines driven by steam and lamps lit by gases.

His home is a chamber of wonders and of industry. If a visitor is to stop in a hallway to light a pipe, for example, a hand bearing a gas-fueled match is likely to extend from what appears to be a marble sculpture to aid in the purpose.

Zala and Jean-Auguste have had seven children together and each of them lives at the family home and participates in one way or another in the construction of Jean-Auguste's inventions or in the design. The oldest is now twenty-six and the youngest is just nine. The main room in his house is the former ball-room which has been converted into a kind of open workshop. At one end is a set of curved, sweeping stairs that descend like arms down each side of the room, meet and open onto the main floor. From the balcony above the stairs, Jean-Auguste can look over the activity in the room. Flames from a burner leap up to heat air to fill a balloon; one of his sons bathes paper in solutions of silver-nitrate, trying to perfect the reproduction of images thereon. Animals and people of all sorts lie in various stages of construction: magicians pause for cards to appear from their tables below; a snake charmer sits by the thousand pieces of her serpent waiting for them to be assembled; an elephant with no cloth on its wiry trunk lifts the appendage skyward and trumpets, momentarily attracting the attention of everyone in the room. There are chuckles, a smattering of applause, and Georges, fourteen years old, takes a bow before the others go back to their work.

Jean-Auguste is guided by his spirit more than anything and sees that as he has aged and as his enquiries into the nature of life and the very meaning of existence have deepened, he has become more and more convinced that there is a great and beautiful pattern at work in the universe. As a scientist, he appreciates its complexity because, although he believes in the pattern, he can see irregularities and exceptions everywhere. He does not believe in social constructions which keep people from believing that they have power to change their lives .

So when he attends mass at the cathedral, it is not to ascend to the tenets of a religion, but to meditate on the richness of life as he knows it.

He has just come from a meeting with officials of the cathedral and the magistrate of the city in which they have agreed to commission him to perform a renovation on the cathedral's clock. The church has recently been returned to the Protestants for the second time in its history, and Austria and France are at war. In the past years, he has spent many hours looking at the stilled clock and he approaches them to suggest that at some point in the future he might be interested in looking into it to see if he could repair or rebuild it, because, as anyone can see, it was once a glorious thing. He has not been thinking about his promise as an eight year old to make the clock work again, but he knows he has been fascinated by it as far back as his memory will take him.

The officials barely let him get a sentence in and cannot control their excitement. The leaders of the city have been looking for a way to distract people from their concerns about the war, and church officials need to convert Catholics and keep them coming to worship at the cathedral. "What we need," a chorus of voices announces as he begins to doubt his participation, "is a miracle."

He stands on the balcony of the ballroom-workshop surveying his family at work. Then he puts his fingers together, places them into his mouth to hold his tongue back, and whistles as loudly as he can. Everyone in the room looks up at once and sees him standing there in his flowing overcoat. He holds onto the banister to lean into the room and speak. "Stop," he says, voice just audible over the burner at the back of the room and the buzz of motors that will not be halted as easily as his children. "I have news."

It takes the entire Stimmler entourage, including Zala and Carina, from 1809 to 1812 to complete the renovation of the clock. Jean-Auguste examines the works and realizes quickly and with some relief that repairing the clock will not be possible. He can keep the case and restore some of the paintings, but when it comes to the mechanism, he must begin at the beginning.

As a scientist and engineer, astronomy has long been of interest to him so it is not difficult to adapt to the work necessary to understand how to calculate and represent time in its many different facets. He has an expert friend in Johann Tobias Bürg, an astronomer from the observatory in Vienna whom he met through Dr. Auenbrugger, and Bürg is pleased to help him in any way.

What surprises Jean-Auguste are the leaps of the imagination required. He has challenged himself just as he was tested when he set out to build the Little Patient so many years before. He is not merely building a device to represent the way time passes, but also to represent the mysteries of the universe. It is as if he has taken a step back and can see that great, glorious design that he has only glimpsed parts of before. Now he is not trying to create *a* life, singular, alone, isolated; he is building something that will represent life *entire*, the whole immense enigma that is nature itself and that excites him down to his toes.

Here, finally, is his chance to make something live.

The other surprise is his new understanding of how time is the standard of meaning which all people subscribe to. It is perfect and imperfect at the same time. How beautiful that the moon, a minute object by celestial standards, can perfectly eclipse the sun from the perspective of a human being standing on earth. What habits of mind that correspondence is responsible for! The sun and the moon are thought of as opposites, so become metaphors for night and day, male and female, good and evil; and yet, from a greater distance, it would be impossible to see any relationship between them at all except, perhaps, that each celestial object is, as Bürg puts it, "a little bit round." Or there is the beautiful incoherence of the rate at which the earth revolves on its axis so that its perfect (though elliptical) passage around the sun does not quite form an even correspondence with an even number of rotations. However, if one calculates the time as the Mayans of Central America did it is possible to see this distortion as part of a very large design as well. In other words, Jean-Auguste realizes, if one waits long enough, the pattern will eventually be completed. It may simply take a few thousand years.

His initial scheme for the clock is to keep the fabulous old statues and to populate the clock with a metropolis of automata so that it will hold the attention of onlookers and will encourage them to stay and contemplate their own lives while they study his fantastic device. As the plans progress, however, he begins to see that the creation of real wonder will be a much slower process.

He begins by gutting the case and taking out every moving part that has made the clock function in the past. Nothing is to be saved. He starts anew but works with the existing structure so that most of the old paintings and statuary are maintained and restored.

He works backward from the slowest movement to the fastest. In front of the clock, he builds a celestial globe that reproduces the movement of five thousand visible stars. This device is something the casual observer might pay little attention to because it looks merely like a standard globe painted with stars rather than continents. Anyone who gets to know the clock well though, will see that the celestial globe is much more than that. The apparent movement of those five thousand stars is charted exactly and individually. Like someone on their back at night watching stars, the globe does not at first appear to be moving. It is only when one looks at it once and then again after several hours that one might see that it is in motion at all. Because the earth revolves around the sun and not around the stars, the measurement for the rotation from star meridian to star meridian is four minutes shorter than the rotation of noon sun to noon sun. It is the measurement of the sidereal day rather than the solar day and this difference must be accounted for in the gears.

Inside the celestial globe, Jean-Auguste includes a wheel-movement to reproduce the gyration of the earth's axis every 25806 years. With this mechanism, only dedicated disciples of the clock will be aware that this particular calculation is taking place.

As was the case with the other two versions of the clock, the main dials measure astronomical movements, since all the units of time depend upon the relationship between earth and other celestial bodies. Jean-Auguste includes new calculations from astronomers. These scientists have measured the irregularities of gravity that make the entire system seem impossibly complicated and imperfect.

His clock shows the opposite: that what seems to be imperfect is flawed only because we do not observe it with enough perspective. It is like looking at the skin of an orange from millimeters away: it appears pocked and strange, whereas, from a distance, all those flaws become a perfect sphere.

He wants some of the works to be visible, so removes panels on both sides of the clock case and replaces them with glass. The windows will allow onlookers to see the brass gear-train mechanisms for the solar and lunar calculations (in the right window) and the ecclesiastical device (in the left) which, on the thirty-first of December each year, activates itself during the night and undertakes the calculations which set the calendar for the solar and lunar cycle, and so allow for the moveable feasts, like the date of Easter Sunday, to be figured. These brass gear-trains are also responsible for activating the leap years.

There is a gear with one missing tooth that will allow for the leap year exception, in which years divisible by four get an extra day *unless* they are also divisible by one hundred in which case the extra day is skipped, *except* for the leap year exception exception: when the year is divisible by *four hundred*, in which case it gets the extra day again. For that calculation, an extra gear is necessary which will turn only once every four hundred years.

There is a calendar dial ten feet around which displays the day and the date and indicates the feast day. Using pinions, ratchets, cams and cam followers, and other devices: pawls, pivots, cranks, levers, and cables, the dial turns once a day. At the end of the year when the ecclesiastical computer activates, tags slide into place to mark Easter Sunday, and the other festival days for the year also shift into alignment. The same dial communicates the changing tides and marks eclipses of the sun and the moon. The mathematics involved are worthy of genius. Making that math tangible in the form of brass systems requires something more, and Jean-Auguste is up to the task. He is Mozart and the clock is his *Jupiter*.

The clock dial is deceptively simple. It has two sets of hands to mark the official time by which commerce in the country functions, and the local time which is about half an hour later. The pendulum that keeps this sort of time runs the entire system.

Above the clock dial is another large circle which is an orrery upon which the movement of the six stars visible to the eye are set in slow motion in relation to the signs of the zodiac. Jean-Auguste includes not only the stars, but also the moons of Jupiter and Saturn. Using the trick he perfected on the Levitating Magician, the planets and the moons appear to be floating freely, so even though their movements are too slow to be observed at a glance, the optical illusion draws a certain degree of attention.

There is a moon which has its own cabinet. Half is covered with gold leaf and half painted with black paint. It rotates slowly on its axis mimicking the phases of the moon in the sky.

The year indicator is a row of numbers, each on a wheel. Several decades later, once automobiles are invented, this contrivance will be known as an odometer. Since each wheel has numbers from 0 to 9, the indicator is good until the year 9999, so no one will have to worry about the system for at least eight thousand years. Jean-Auguste suggests that if the clock is still functioning then (and he sees no reason why it shouldn't be) then a '1' might be painted before the year indicator giving the whole thing another ten thousand years to operate.

Inside the pendulum tower: bells, an aurora of them. The carillon includes a rotating program of tunes which works on local time so as not to compete with the bells in the cathedral tower which are rung according to official time. The chimes play only on Sundays and only before the first mass so no one but the devout early risers get a chance to hear them. It is Jean-Auguste's way of encouraging people out of their beds.

Then there are the automata. He knows that the figures he includes will attract the most attention and that many, perhaps most people, will notice only them, but he also knows that those who are truly drawn to the clock will see that the automata are merely a surface demonstration of the works going on inside the housing.

Under the glass cabinets with the sun and moon gears, there is a room like a cavern which Jean-Auguste fills with monks, four of them labouring over manuscripts, writing out and illustrating in careful hand, the book of Genesis. Each works on a fourth of the manuscript in one minute spurts, four times a day, and they move so slowly that the scrolls they write upon need only be collected and collated at the end of each year and replenished with fresh paper so they may write out their story again.

Under the ecclesiastical computer, to balance out the monks and as a tribute to science, is an astronomer, modelled on Bürg, who moves from his telescope to his drawing table, plotting out the movements of the planets on a large celestial map. He too works for only short periods so his charting is painstaking.

Beside the clock dial, Jean-Auguste places two cherubs: a tribute to the first clock. The one on the left removes an arrow from his quiver and strikes a bell once every fifteen minutes to announce the passing of the quarter hour, and as he is the first to move, he beckons the attention of parish-ioners for the more animated displays on the hour. The one on the right upturns an hourglass every half-hour.

Above the dials, there is a procession of apostles which happens at midday. From a chamber behind the clock, a door opens and each of the apostles moves across the front of the cabinet, walking lifelike to kneel and bow before Christ who blesses each in turn before they proceed along. As a reminder of human frailty, there is a cockerel atop the gear pillar which flaps its wings and crows three times during the procession of the apostles to remind of the story of Peter's denial.

Throughout the planning process, Jean-Auguste tries to strike the right balance between religious decorum and his own somewhat impertinent sensibility. He builds a scene to the right of the planet dial in which Eve is tempted by the serpent, and he has the snake climb rather suggestively up through her smock and out the neckline, emerging with an apple he did not have when he began his ascent.

As a tribute to earlier times, he uses a space above Eve to create a moving tableau that is an homage to the animal world. It includes a peacock which fans its tail impressively before a small waterfall while a peahen produces a golden egg and sets to brooding on her nest. After one lunar month, the egg cracks open revealing a young peafowl. There are two bears which emerge from a hidden "den" behind the waterfall in the early spring and set to picking berries by the stream that flows from the waterfall, and there is a rabbit in a warren which, through the clever use of trick mirrors, appears to multiply right before the observers' eyes until there is a plague of rabbits overrunning the little forest crèche.

At first, Jean-Auguste has plans for an elaborate nativity scene to be activated on Christmas evening, but he realizes that if he is to keep the daily procession of the apostles, then he can not also have a nativity. It is a big clock but there is still room for merely one Christ upon it. As a compromise, he creates a star of Bethlehem which begins to glow more brightly on the celestial globe a week before Christmas, and which gets brighter and brighter as the days go on until it is nearly impossible to look directly at it without fear of some lasting damage to the eye.

Toward the crown of the clock, Jean-Auguste includes musicians. There are, naturally, a flute player and a drummer, and there is also a young woman who plays harpsichord. Beside the flautist he builds a lute player, harpist, and violinist and then adds a wind section with a trumpet, a tuba, and an oboe.

The days of the week are represented not far from the monks by a procession of gods in chariots named after the days of the week. Saturn, for example, Samstag or Saturday, is a vicious old man in a chariot who devours his own child as he is pulled by raging dragons who expel smoke from their snouts. These are set into motion at the close of each day and are some of the only automata who do not respect the period of evening rest which silences many of the other features of the clock.

Most of the automata are set into motion once a day or once a week, depending upon what it is they represent. The apostles move at noon, the weekday gods at midnight. Some of the figures dance only Sundays and others on feast days, but Jean-Auguste has also built in some great surprises.

In common years, the New Year will be a special occasion, marked by a circus performance. The painting of Copernicus on the weight-drive pillar will slide sideways, revealing a miniature ring master who will crack his long whip as lions emerge from their cages and approach. Clowns will walk tightropes, juggle whining kittens, and produce a half-moon from a magic hat.

On leap years, the circus performance will be followed by a display of blossoms in the garden at Eve's feet. At midnight, the leaves of an angel's trumpet plant will unfold around Eve's ankles and then the blossom will emerge and flower. Even later, at three in the morning, a moonflower will appear, and then a sequence of other blossoms through the New Year's Day, each emitting its own scent which will fill the transept with perfume. The last to blossom will be a small patch of pink night phlox, the tiny flowers of which will end the performance with their honey-vanilla scent.

When he is long dead and the clock is nearly one hundred years old, it will be the year 1900. When that date rolls around, and to mark every new century thereafter, a door in the crown of the clock will open at midnight on the night of the last day of December, 1899 and a flock of swallows he has built will be released to flutter up to the top of the cathedral pillars and then to plunge and swoop around the great spaces of the altar and the transepts.

Jean-Auguste knows that what might be at least as important as the tricks his machine can accomplish, are the stories that are told about it. This is a realization that both fuels his desire to have his clock noticed and also his criticism of too literal belief in scripture. As ancient events become tales, then legends, then myths, the progress toward mystery involves the way things are reported as much as what happened. To this end, he envisions surprises. With no way for observers to anticipate what will happen, he builds in a number of temporal events that will seem to happen at random.

One of these events is the spectacle of the creation of the world. At fifteen minutes past ten on the morning of June tenth, 1826 (for no particular reason except Jean-Auguste's belief that someone will be near to watch), a gear will engage and another one of the paintings, a representation of the Last Judgement, will slide over and unveil a blank landscape surrounded by darkness. A light will begin to brighten high in the cabinet, then water will well up and before it has a chance to cascade out of the chamber, a landscape will rise to contain it. On the hills, fruit trees, cherries and apricots, will sprout and bear fruit, and then a whale will appear in the 'sea' to spout a breath of air. Living creatures on land will be represented only by cattle which will eat fruit from the trees, and Eve, over on the other side of the clock, will take a big bite out of her apple and (this is an example of Jean-Auguste's irreverence), on this one occasion, she will wink unrepentant at the observers.

At other times, the story of the ten virgins, the parable of the pearl, and the riot in Ephesus will be enacted by surprise, and so the Wolsenburg Clock will develop its own legends. People will say that they saw things which no one can verify and which no one else for generations will see again, and in this way, Jean-Auguste's creation will rise even higher in the imaginations of those faithful to his clock.

All of this, magic tricks, reproducing rabbits, levitating planets, and flying sparrows, he can accomplish with mathematics and gears, but as the clock is nearing completion, there is one thing that has him thwarted. Inconspicuously set behind the hour dial of the old clock, there was a marble urn which, he is told, holds the relics of

St. Peter with which the cathedral was founded. He has had to remove the urn to make space for his cherubs and does not now know how to incorporate it into his plan.

Though in many ways the design of the clock, the carved stone and wood of the case, the paintings, and his additions, are a mash of various styles and designs, the clock has a kind of pleasing unity. Anywhere he considers placing the phoenix seems like the wrong place. He simply cannot see where it should go. He is told that it has been part of the clock since the cathedral was first consecrated and unless he would like to rail against half a millennium of tradition, he should find somewhere suitable to incorporate it. So he does.

The clock is finished by the summer of 1812 and is blessed and set into motion on St. Augustine's day.

Jean-Auguste lives well into a century which unfolds with both wonder and horror. He is ninety years old when he dies. The American civil war is beginning, Louis Pasteur publishes a paper on the germ theory of disease, Charles Dickens writes *Great Expectations.*

He lies in state in his casket in the south transept of the cathedral. While his family, friends, and admirers pass by to pay their last respects, a choir featuring representations of each of his seven children and of Carina and Zala, springs forth from the crown of the clock above the musicians. There is a click. The first notes come from the youngest figure, and then the others sing harmony. Their mechanical voices produce a version of the Ave Maria that makes everyone in the great building smile.

Epilogue

When the third clock was inaugurated, Jean-Auguste Stimmler was forty-one years old. He had half a century to live with his invention. I have managed to spend fully sixty-one years with the clock, and yet, in many ways, I have only just begun to be acquainted with it.

Through good fortune, rather than healthy living, Wolsenburg has continued to be my home. My university in Canada had seen my time away during the war as an extension of my leave and offered me my post back in 1945, but I chose instead to stay and I live here now, with Leesa, who is yet my wife, although some days I cannot be sure where she gets the patience.

I still do not know what it is Josias Stimmler saw in me, but he seemed to know instinctively that I would be willing and even able to take over his role. He was the last of his line and told me simply that he had known his own life would not last too long, so began watching those who came to look at the clock, trusting that the right person would appear to take over from him. Who was I to argue with providence?

He died in 1942 giving me one more reason to reconcile my accidentally being in Wolsenburg.

Leesa and I have a good life. We live across the square from the cathedral in the roomy attic apartment of a building that is six hundred years old. I have come to have an appreciation for things that have stood the test of time. We were not able to be married until after the war, but we found this place and were able to purchase it after the treaties were signed and my fortunate friend, a man I had known merely for a number of hours at the conference in London so long ago, was returned, gratefully, to his flat in which I had spent the war years.

So as to allow the city to get some rest, and because the community no longer needs a reminder of the time every hour through the night, the cathedral bells are silent from eleven in the evening until seven in the morning, and they begin and end with a peel that lasts ten minutes. The first night I spent with Leesa in our flat under the roof, it was summer and our window was open. I do not think it is proper for me to provide details here of the nature of our physical engagement, but suffice it to say that when the bells began to ring out that evening, echoing into our chamber as if our bed were in the very bell tower itself, the sound of those great chimes was utterly fitting to our state of being, and it was as if winged creatures poured into the room with the sound to bless our union.

I was convinced that we had conceived a child that night, and for a month and a half afterwards every sign suggested that I was correct, but it was not to be. And still we remain without our own child. Leesa said we shouldn't be concerned.

She was surrounded by children all day in her work at the theatre. In fact, she continues to be so surrounded because although she has found in her adolescent niece her own apprentice, still she performs with her puppets in the theatre in the garden. For many years she said, "If a child is in our future, it will arrive in good time," and although no child blessed us, we continue, perhaps recklessly, to believe that we have a future. I carried Leesa over the threshold in her white dress on our wedding night and then nailed the train to the floor so she would not, could not, abandon me as I declined over the decades. We have forged friendships and maintained them only to have them fade as we have aged and those around us have fallen into disrepair and eventually quit chiming.

Meanwhile, I maintain the clock to the extent that it must be maintained. I reset the weights once a week on Mondays and occasionally I need to perform some small service to the mechanism, which most often has to do with cleaning out dust, or other detritus that has somehow found its way among the gears. And I maintain the cosmetic elements of the clock, polishing and repainting with a ceaseless and careful hand.

After the war, I took over Stimmler's role as tour guide. It was my idea to get the cathedral to sell tickets for the noon chimes and the procession of the apostles. At first they were reluctant because it meant clearing out the cathedral an hour before in order to make sure to collect from the entire audience. I convinced them, however, that people feel better about things they must pay for than things which come to them for free. Besides, I said, we could easily make enough from just modest ticket sales to pay my salary and to keep the clock in fresh paint as long as it needs it.

Now it is my show. I herd people out of the cathedral, take my own slow time to sell tickets by the transept door from a little wicket I had built for the purpose, collect the tickets when again I open the doors, and then tell the story of the clock in the twenty minutes it takes to get everyone settled before the first chimes ring out. My bones are not as crackling as Stimmler's, but they ache with arthritis and pop when I break from a long sit in the pews.

On a good day, there will be four hundred people gathered around to hear my speech. In winter when tourists are scarce, there might be just twenty but I give them the same version of the tale that I give big crowds. I took on gladly my role as keeper of the clock and holder of its stories; what better way to bear witness to wonder until such time as my own heart might stop ticking?

I have seen from this perspective what it is that Josias Stimmler saw from his. Most people are impressed easily by the Wolsenburg clock. Some, however, seem disappointed after the cock crows his last note. I am not sure what more they want. Do they think the vault of the ceiling should open, a white light shine down, and angels come to bear them up to heaven for an audience with their Maker? Perhaps for some, if it is not Disneyland, it cannot be magic.

And then there are others in whose eyes I recognize a certain light. I have seen them come and go. Most often they are children. Like Leesa, I find myself surrounded by them these days. School groups from all over Europe pour into the cathedral by the dozens, and I see the full spectrum of children in them. There are the bored and cynical who would remain closed to the most extraordinary things. One could wave a magic wand to make their bus disappear and they would yawn thinking it was "just some trick" that did not bear thinking about. Other children are the products of the Ritalin generation, either talking well beyond the speeds of the autobahn, or gazing with glazed, drug-coated eyes.

In every group though, I see at least one child: she or he will be the one who is suddenly separated from companions because of the way his or her gaze is caught by the clock. This is a child who will disappear into reverie caught in the spell of the great machine. When I give my lecture, it is these children I feel that I am addressing and no others.

Do you know something I like very much? I like having a big crowd in front of the clock and explaining what it is they are about to see when the gears engage. And then I like to glance through the audience for those people who can not stop themselves from looking at their own wristwatches to judge when the show is about to start.

I have stood next to a couple right in front of the great clock of Wolsenburg and heard a man ask his wife if she knew what time it was. He was not a blind fellow, only a little dim. As I was debating with myself about whether I might say anything about his innocence from knowledge, the woman gave him a loving look of understanding and both burst out laughing at the question, relieving me from any further worry about the subject.

We depend on our gauges of time now in ways even Jean-Auguste Stimmler could not have imagined. And yet one of my most fervent beliefs is that such complex measures of time are unnecessary. The simple method of using variable solar time — that the day begins when the sun rises and ends when the sun sets — is to me a more sensible approach to living in time. Perhaps what humans need more than anything is not atomic clocks that help us keep more and more precise track of time, but less complicated lives so the measurements would again matter less.

It is not breaking down time into more minute fractions that will help us understand the world around us, it is seeing our place in the great, slow unfolding of things that to me is a truly holy enterprise.

This new year marks the beginning of the second millennium. There is talk all around of the end of the world. People have stocked their shelves with emergency supplies in case all things grind to a halt when the clock strikes twelve. They fail to remember that the world has ended at least twice already in my own lifetime and still we are here. And yet the clock ticks.

I have gathered together a small group of people with me and brought them into the cathedral before midnight to worship whatever it is that seems to keep air flowing into and out of our lungs and blood flowing into and out of our hearts. Some are nearly as old as me — like the clergy I have worked with for decades; others are young, fresh people who have simply won their way into the audience by asking me enough questions as they took my tour. Included in the young group are both men and women, artists, writers, art students, and budding engineers. My hope is that one of them will be my replacement some day and my suspicion is that the most likely candidate will reveal him or herself to me through a glance or gesture I will simply recognize, and my belief is, it will happen on the turn of the new millennium.

When I was his apprentice, Josias Stimmler taught me everything he knew about the clock's history and showed me all he knew about its works. But last year, as I was engaged in refinishing an oak panel behind the astrolabe, I dislodged a spring on a trap door which opened to reveal what I knew instantly to be the phoenix urn that is the reliquary for the church. It was resting on a platform at what is likely the very centre of the clock and it seemed to me that Stimmler had indeed found the right place for it as the heart of the device.

I was able to correct the spring and re-engage it as it was. Knowing the clock as I now do, I have faith that one day, this trap door and the urn will play some vital role in the display. I will not be surprised if, on this, the evening of the new millennium, the door will open and indeed the vaults of heaven will unfold, or some great resurrection might take place — St. Peter or some other angel will emerge alive for a second time from the clock's works. Perhaps a star will rise into the night sky and Leesa's withered old beautiful womb will produce a miraculous (though not immaculate) child. Perhaps that star will signal a second coming, an end, a beginning? Who knows what spectacles await us?

It is fifteen minutes before midnight and the little cherub with his arrow has just struck the bell. There are two dozen of us here, and all I could promise them was that the clock would be sure to make the new millennium memorable. Leesa is beside me, holding my hand as I look upwards. I believe she is more excited than I and I love her for that.

Jay Ruzesky

As for me, I am content to wait quietly for whatever may come my way, feeling confident now that this life I have been living is a gift to me, and fortunate that all the wonders I am lucky enough to bear witness to make me feel chosen.

ACKNOWLEDGEMENTS

The Leighton Colony at the Banff Centre for the Arts provided space and inspiration as did John Lent and my friends at Wayword, Protection Island; thanks to the BC Arts Council and the Canada Council for the Arts; and special thanks to my sharp readers, especially PK Page, Carol Matthews, and the Gentlemen of the Gentlemen's Fiction Club — Bill Gaston, Mike Matthews, Bill Stenson, and Terence Young.

An excerpt of this novel first appeared in *Event* Magazine. Thanks to the editors and staff there for continued support and encouragement.

I would also like to acknowledge my editor at Thistledown Press, Seán Virgo, who cared for this book as if it were a favoured child and helped it grow up in the space of a few short months. I offer gratitude to everyone at the press for believing in this book.

Although some of the characters in this novel resemble historical figures, their representations here are fictional treatments and they are in no way intended to be accurate biographical portrayals.

Readers may, as I did, find the following resources useful to learn more about the development of astronomical clocks, automata, and alchemy:

Bailly, Christian. *Automata: the Golden Age*. London: Sotheby's Publications, 1987.

Chapuis, Alfred, and Edmund Droz. *Automata: A Historical and Technological Study*. Trans. Alec Reid. Neuchatel, Switzerland: Editions du Griffon, 1958.

King, Henry. *Geared to the Stars: The Evolution of Planetariums, Orreries, and Astronomical Clocks*. Toronto: University of Toronto Press, 1978.

Lehni, Roger. *Strasbourg Cathedral's Astronomical Clock*. Trans. R. Beaumont-Craggs. Saint-Ouen, FR: Éditions La Goélette, 2002.

Martin, Sean. *Alchemy and Alchemists*. Harpenden, GBR: Pocket Essentials, 2001.

Photo: Hana Ruzesky-Bashford

JAY RUZESKY is a well-known poet whose work has received international recognition. *The Wolsenburg Clock*, is his first novel. Ruzesky lives on Vancouver Island where he teaches at Vancouver Island University and serves on the board of the literary journal, The *Malahat Review*.